12

D1384599

The
Autobiography
of
CASSANDRA
Princess & Prophetess
of
Troy

MIDDLEBURY COLLEGE LIBRARY

Ursule Molinaro

ARCHER EDITIONS PRESS

PS
3525
O 2152
A9

1/1980
Rev'l

THE AUTOBIOGRAPHY OF CASSANDRA

First Edition

Copyright 1979 by Ursule Molinaro
Printed in the United States of America
All rights reserved. No part of this book
or parts of the works thereof may be reproduced
or transmitted in any form by any means, electronic
or mechanical, including photocopying and recording,
or by any information storage or retrieval system,
without permission in writing from the publisher.

"Letter to Apollo" was previously published in
Contemporary Quarterly, 2:3, 1977.

Library of Congress Cataloging in Publication Data

Molinaro, Ursule.
    The autobiography of Cassandra, princess & prophetess
of Troy.

    1.   Cassandra—Fiction.   I.   Title.
PZ4.M722Au   (PS3535.02152)   813'.5'4   79-1410
ISBN 0-89097-013-0

Design by Wanda Hicks

To New York City
May it fare better than
Cassandra's Troy.

With thanks to CAPS
& to the URBAN CORPS
for assigning me a student: Dean Schwaab
whose intelligent research helped to make
the transition from a project to a book.

FOOTNOTE

The personality of Cassandra has been assembled from many contradictory legends, & from images of her on surviving pieces of art.

Her conviction that the fall of Troy would bring about barbaric times & establish the social demotion of women for centuries to come is an interpretation of historical findings & their interpreters.

Autobiographies tend to mythologize their subject matter in an effort to adapt past facts to what looks like the truth at the time of writing. The autobiography of a mythological figure is no exception. This novel hopes to make an unbelieved prophetess into a believable person.

To the frowning researcher &/or Homer-addict, I'd like to quote M. de Talleyrand's remark at the Congress of Vienna: "Messieurs, appuyons-nous sur les principes. Ils finiront bien par ceder." (Gentlemen, let us lean on our principles. They will eventually give.)

A metallic smell of blood grabbed me by the throat as we turned the last corner in the slowly climbing road, & the palace of Mycenae appeared in full view, streaked with afternoon sunshine.

I started coughing.

Agamemnon, beaming & paternal, pounded me on the back. The boys wanted to know if "Mommy was going to vomit". They had been seasick during most of the crossing, their father holding their livid foreheads, while I laughed at Greek victors dropping overboard like giant crabs. At Ajax the Locrian who had raped me during the last hours of Troy. While Athena's vengeful waves played with them for a few acrobatic moments before swallowing them up.

I shook my head; cough-laughing: No. I'd never felt better.

Agamemnon hugged my shoulders.

We're home: he said: Home!

He got down on his knees & kissed the earth. When he stood up, his eyes were wet with tears. Of joy.

I had seen it all before, during endless visions. Which accelerated & overlapped as the end drew closer. My deja vu life. I was impatient to get it over with. For all of us.

It was the 13th day of January. That night the moon would be full. I would not see it. Not one of us would. I was 33 years old, but the last ten years felt as though each had lasted ten times ten years.

Being murdered was like an operation: I told myself: A few ugly moments, & no more pain.

I had not reckoned with the undying curse of resentment. That has preserved my memory, intact like a fly trapped in a tear of amber. Excluded from metamorphosis. Making me rehearse each incident   over & over   as I search for reasons behind my unfair fate. & discover unsuspected motivations   tie-ins ambiguities. Contradictions.

The story of my life has long spidery roots that have spun a cocoon around the truth. I, who could foretell the future, find it difficult to disentangle the past.

In retrospect, my warnings & the events which led to the fall of Troy look identical. The outline has blended with the outcome, leaving no margin for alternatives. But while Troy was

still standing —on a site on which six cities had
stood & fallen! before her: as I kept telling
my closed-eared compatriots— everyone but me
saw a million other possibilities. Except the
ugly facts which I foretold.

Events grow from a seed, like everything
else connected with life. & like everything else,
they ripen at the speed of their species.
Outlines of disaster   which were often
preceded by a foul odor   usually manifested
sooner than favorable circumstances. (Which I
had the privilege of foreseeing only for enemies
of Troy. For Odysseus. & disconcertingly
for my twin brother Helenus.)
By human time, the immortals seemed to
live very slowly. The way we must seem to be
living   unendingly   to the short-lived
creatures. This may explain why divine
assistance often took the form of retribution,
instead of prevention. Yet, when their interest
had been aroused, the gods' intervention could
be faster than fear.
It was as though our past, present, &
future co-existed on Olympus. Every once in a
while a cloud would part, & the seer could catch
a glimpse of what lay ahead.
But even then it was usually impossible
to discern the total situation until it had become
practically inescapable. A blatant detail   like a
beautiful woman, or the flashing of an ax
might stand out with blinding clarity, but
out of context. Falling into place only as it
happened.

After the fact, the cumulative effect of a million minor details looked natural enough. But foreseeing them   speeded up & condensed   made them appear like images of phantasy. Even to the seer, whose interpretation was not necessarily understandable even to himself.

This is why people complain about the ambiguity of oracles. Which they consult mainly to be told that they can follow their predilections, & everything will be all right.

It is seldom the case.

It may seem heroic   or perverse   that, knowing what I knew, I did not try to save at least myself. But where could I have fled? Who would have taken me in? Apollo's revenge had cast a subtle net around me, ostracizing me, by my uncommunicable knowledge. The men who sought my hand & died for my sake on the walls of Troy would not have braved preordination, if they had listened to the forecast of my fate. To the man in the street I had become the hard-luck princess, whose contact he feared to be contagious. My embarrassed father threatened to lock me up if I didn't keep quiet. He didn't fulfill his threat, & I continued to foretell what I could not prevent.

There were moments when I thought of hanging myself. From a tree outside Apollo's shrine in Thymbra. —Spitting back at Apollo.— But I, too, had been raised in the belief that our fate was preordained. Something was bound to

4

interfere with my unprogrammatic death.
Apollo himself might gleefully cut me down,
forcing me to live out my allotted time. Worse
off than before, perhaps, with a bitten-off
tongue, or a dangling neck, my chin grazing my
chest. Grotesquely continuing to warn my city
& her people.

Whom I would be betraying, by
committing suicide: I also thought. Illogically;
because my belief in preordination had not
freed me from hope & fear. I kept hoping
against hope that someone   my brother
Hector, my anguished wavering mother
   would start listening to me after my first
predictions came true.

But they had not listened while I made
them. Usually they'd run out of the room   or
push me out   when they noticed my eyes
turning upward, at the beginning of a trance.

Each new vision used to terrify me as
much as the disaster itself. In spite of additional
sensations which I had not foreseen. Sometimes
I'd tell myself what the others were telling
me: That I was hallucinating. Because I had
weak blood, perhaps, for which I was made to
drink vile-tasting herb teas my old nurse
brewed for me. Why should I alone know the
truth? What I saw was too horrible to come
true!

The slaying of 3 of my brothers.

My gout-ridden father limping into
useless combat.

Polyxena, my spoiled beautiful sister, sacrificed across Achilles' grave.

My severed head skidding across sticky palace tiles, my trailing hair rinsed red by my own blood.

Agamemnon collapsing in his bath, a grimace of disbelief on his paternal face.

My children's heads thudding to the ground like pale melons...

It was too much. For too long. Evil had to spend itself: I tried to rationalize: at least before it reached my children.

I would have had to prevent their conception to save them from being murdered.

But during that brief instant   on the windy September afternoon in Thymbra, when I gave myself to Agamemnon   I saw nothing.

I did smell a dank odor that seemed to come seeping from the temple floor. But I attributed it to a dead snake. To the anger of a god who had perhaps watched a mortal, being let in where His Godship had been refused entry. On his own sacred homeground. The thought gave me a certain pleasure, for which Agamemnon took delighted credit. Much of the happiness he found with me was derived from similar misunderstandings.

I don't know if every mortal's life is determined geographically. If there is one particular place where the mortal goes as though by appointment, & meets his/her

6

destiny. Over & over; good & bad alike, as seems to have been my case in Thymbra. In Apollo's temple, which stood outside the city walls, a short climb up the northern slope of Mount Ida. During the siege, it was used by Trojans & Greeks alike, who'd often run into each other, making offerings to bribe divine partiality.

Agamemnon had crept up behind me. He remarked that I was not sacrificing to Apollo. I said I had sacrificed to Apollo   once & for all   a number of years ago. But he wasn't listening. He had followed me to the temple many times before: he said. For months he had watched me walk up the slope. He had arrived at the conclusion that he loved me.

A man has to reach the age of forty to know what he loves: he said.

He was an unhappily married man closer to fifty than to forty, actually   who considered himself a favorite of the gods. He was disarmingly determined to make me happy in spite of the wretched war between us. That had, however, contrived our meeting'... He wanted to 'get it over with, & take me 'home'...'.

I think I let Agamemnon love me because I felt that he, too, had been earmarked a loser. The richest & most powerful of all our neighboring kings, & the future conqueror of my city, but a loser.

Who still thought that he was winning when Clytemnestra filled his bath. My heart flooded with compassion every time I looked into his trusting face. We belonged to the same species. I was the lame leading the blind...

To his gory end. Which I was shown soon after, in a dream. In great detail, neatly superimposed upon the idyllic background of two laughing little boys. The twins I was going to bear, Pelops & Teledamus, who looked exactly like their mother. Two disconcerting versions of my more & more solemn face.

But I, too, had been a laughing child. At thirteen I'd still been known as 'the golden princess with the ready smile'.

I was the only blonde among Hecabe's daughters.

Until my mishap with Apollo I used to think that I would remain a virgin, like my protectress Athena. The goddess of conscious knowledge.

—& of prophecy. Which never was the monopoly of Apollo. It was from Athena that Tiresias, the most respected of Greek seers, received his prophetic gift. After she blinded him, for an unintentional glimpse of her bathing body.

I wanted to be useful. I wanted to become an oracular priestess, & help my contemporaries live better lives as they listened to my predictions. & heeded my warnings about pitfalls in their fate.

—Which were tests, I used to think, sent
us by·the gods to make us stronger.

But when Apollo spat into my mouth &
made me unbelievable, he drowned my faith. I
stopped believing that the gods had the good of
mortals in mind. & that our misfortunes were
selfmade; the consequences of our disobedience
or lack of understanding. I began to think that
the gods were solely interested in themselves.
In power, for which they seemed to be eternally
scheming. It was a wise mortal who managed
to live unnoticed.

Since then I've come to realize that gods
wear out. It is the office that remains immortal.

The ruling symbol of one culture is
declared taboo by its conquerors. & to the
conquerors' conquerors it becomes untouchable.
Obscene.

After Apollo slaughtered the Python &
established his own oracular shrine in the womb-
cave of Delphi, his priestesses   —whom he
chose virginal, but pregnancy-proof, in case
of rape; spinsters past the age of fertility—
were known as pythonesses. Who prophesied
from tripods covered with serpent skin,
& kept serpent bones in reliquaries. An era
later, the sacred serpent became a filthy snake.

& priestesses became witches, as women
were removed from 'office'. & placed upon
pedestals, out of the way of decisions. Pale
madonnas that fluttered ghostlike behind their

former thrones. & were told to kneel: by
fathers / husbands / owners. Who grew in
stature as women shrank to wenches, whose
contact became debilitating to the master sex.
Unclean.

Of all the gods of Greek antiquity, Apollo
has gained the most from posthumous
reputation. (If the word 'posthumous' may be
applied to a one-time Immortal.) No one
remembers that his many skills   prophecy /
healing / music / law   were taken over from
less well-remembered gods & goddesses.
Whom he had occasionally killed, in the process
of robbing them.
Legend has turned him into the great god
of civilization, & speaks with reverence of an
Apollonian society'.
Perhaps his slaying of the female Python
did mark the end of a society. One in which
women used to be wise, & men muscled, & all
children legitimate.
& thereby did initiate a new society. One
that was ruled by men.
Whose gratitude rewrote history.
Making it almost impossible to disinter what
actually happened from under layers of father
worship, & hero flattery, & retroactive laws.
Truth   which was my life-long obsession
(& obsesses me still)   appears to be even more
evasive in retrospect.
—& if possible even less popular. I'm
sure that men who may happen to read me

today will dismiss my findings with an
indignant shrug.

It has taken me   an experienced
seer   several millennia after the fact to arrive
at the conclusion that the seed of Troy's
destruction was sown inadvertently.
The day Gaia   the Great Mother
Herself   expressed concern about over-
population in our area of the earth, & asked
Zeus to help her reform human breeding habits
which were beginning to threaten the balance
of life on earth.
& just as inadvertently, on that same day,
the Great Mother relinquished Her exclusive
authority when she appealed to a male deity for
cooperation.
The Great Mother knew that one
principle alone cannot remodel nature. It can
impose its will, but if it does   as men began to
do, following Apollo's divine example, while I
was still alive & Troy still standing, & have
continued doing ever since   the earth falls ill.
& lingers on through several millennia, while
vermin gradually conquer all other forms of
life. Until they also die, having devoured the last
life form they fed on.
The Great Mother probably had not
expected any opposition from the male
principle. Which had never opposed her before.
Whose dormant ambition   to bring about a
shift of emphasis, from equality to male
predominence; from Moon to Sun   she

11

probably could not imagine, in her universality.

Perhaps Zeus was unconsciously expressing this dormant ambition when he disagreed with the Great Mother's reform proposals:

To take the pride out of parenthood by setting a divine example of conjugal continence. & replace kinship with friendship.

To raise the love level from the loins to heart & head, making man feel ashamed of seeking solace for the animal loneliness of his flesh.

To impose a mating season, if moral measures failed, & slant the desires of the obstinate toward members of the same sex, for a couple of generations, until the threatened balance was restored.

Zeus agreed only to the last part. The introduction of homosexuality appealed to him, but as an extension rather than as a restriction, or a replacement.

He refused to deprive mortal men of his own foremost pleasure. He preferred to make them kill each other, & keep breeding.

Which was the more expedient counterproposal of the Great Mother's daughter Themis, whom Zeus immediately consulted on the problem.

—Themis may still have been Zeus' wife at that time   long before my lifetime although he continued to ask Themis' advice even after his marriage to Hera.

—Which became the divine battleground for the beginning power struggle between the sexes.—

Unlike Hera, Themis was as yet unmotivated by wifely jealousy. Perhaps she still felt secure enough in her goddess position to think that it was harmless to indulge Zeus. Whose not always Olympian concern with mortal procreation may have amused her, the way the ruling sex is sometimes amused by the frivolous playfulness of the other.

Or perhaps she thought that her Great Mother's patience with the haphazardly breeding human race was a waste of   more modern   time. Killing & continued breeding was a faster, lazier solution.

Which became the signal for all the gods on Olympus to start polishing their dormant ambitions. & for mortal men, whose muscles assume heroic proportions, in times of war.

For which a pretext is readily found. Far more readily than incentives for moral evolution.

Patient self-improvement looks far less glamorous   even to mortal women   than sex & violence.

I must have been six, maybe six & a half years old— I had as yet not received my prophetic gift— when Thetis married Peleus. But I remember her wedding as though I had

been invited; together with all the gods, &
almost all the goddesses.

It was considered quite a come-down for
a River daughter, granddaughter of the Ocean,
to marry a mere mortal. Zeus himself had
courted Thetis at one time, after his separation
from Themis, & before his marriage to Hera. &
so had his brother Poseidon, who claimed
priority, based on a common bond of water.

Finally, the two divine brothers had
consulted an oracle, each hoping for a
confirmation of his wishes. (Which proves   to
me   that even divine omniscience can be
obstructed by personal hopes or fears.) But
when they were told that Thetis' son would
surpass his father in immortal glory, both gods
hurriedly withdrew.

Not long afterwards, Zeus married his
sister Hera.

It was at Thetis' wedding party that Eris,
the goddess of discord, threw the fateful apple
'to the Fairest', that was to become the pretext
for ten years of war which ended in the
destruction of my city.

—Thetis' son was Achilles, who slew my
brother Hector. & my youngest brother
Troilus, of whom I had been told in a vision that
Troy would never fall to the Greeks if he
reached the age of twenty. & my two halfbrothers, Lycaon & Mestor.

Of course Eris may have been acting on her own, merely crashing a party from which she had been excluded.

The idea of a beauty contest   between Hera, Athena, & Aphrodite   is altogether in keeping with the character of a goddess of discord.

Whom a bride might understandably not invite.

It is equally understandable that Zeus squirmed when the three competing goddesses confronted him. & that he delegated the role of judge to the first mortal who caught his eye: an insignificant young shepherd who was tending Trojan flocks on Mount Ida. Alexander, who was as brave as he was beautiful. & had perhaps caught Zeus'   or another god's   eye before, chasing cattle thieves.

Everything may have happened 'genuinely'; the way I heard it told as a little girl. When I had not yet received my gift of prophecy, & could not yet see beyond what I heard.

It may have been only after the insignificant young shepherd's judgment   in favor of Aphrodite   that Zeus saw his opportunity to rebalance life on earth by a blood bath, & seized it. & began elaborating.

On the other hand, the throwing of the apple may have been suggested to Eris by another, lesser god. A god who had made it his practice to incorporate his own schemes into the plans of others. & may have derived a

15

feeling of security from discord among those others. Especially among goddesses.

Who may also have drawn Zeus' embarrassed attention to the insignificant young shepherd. ...My older brother Paris, as it turned out later. Whom all of us had thought dead. Renamed Alexander —a man who fights off men— by the other shepherds who admired his courageous bouts with cattle thieves. & his uncommon good looks.

Paris was supposed to have died a few hours after he was born   twenty-four years earlier   done away with by one of my father's herdsmen. Since my father had been unable to do away with the baby himself, after my pregnant mother dreamt that she was carrying a flaming firebrand under her heart that would destroy us all.

Which was what Hera vowed to do, when her judge's royal origins were discovered.

Hera considered herself THE TOTAL WOMAN. A perfect blend of the MOTHER, the VIRGIN, & the WHORE, which later   male scholars have defined as: THE FEMALE TRINITY. Suggesting that the three goddesses: Hera (the mother), Athena (the virgin— although mainly WISDOM), & Aphrodite (the ... seductress) were representing the three aspects of woman which confront a man at Paris' age, when he feels obliged to make a choice.

(The same female trinity allegedly wept at the grave of Jesus, the founder of a

16

later   Christian   religion.)

Hera   who occasionally borrowed
Aphrodite's magic belt to reattach the
philandering Zeus   was outraged by my
brother's choice.   Which did not only deny her
seductiveness, but rated seductiveness as the
highest quality of woman.

—Seductiveness was to become the only
quality of certain women, in the 'Apollonian
society'.   Which considered breeding the only
quality of all the other women.   & demoted the
wise virgin to an old maid.—

Hera vowed to 'wipe the Trojan race off
the map'.

Which may also have been the tacit vow
of a less outspoken   quietly ambitious   god.
Who may have had long-standing reasons for
spoiling Thetis' wedding.   & for enjoying the
sight of Hera blistering before Aphrodite.

& the sight of my ruined city.   That may
have looked to him like his long-coveted chance
to replace Zeus.

Zeus had kept in touch with Thetis, after
running out on her: & Thetis must have
remained fond of Zeus   more than of Poseidon;
or at least jealous of Hera   because it was
Thetis who denounced the plot to unseat Zeus
which Hera had instigated, as a revenge for his
infidelities.

—With the help of Poseidon.   & of
Apollo.   Both of whom Zeus sent down to
earth, after the plot was discovered.   To do

17

penance in the service of a mortal, as punishment for their subversion.

The place on earth happened to be Troy.

Poseidon built the walls of my city   god-made walls which could not be destroyed by mortal hands, only by trickery; by treason while Apollo tended my grandfather's flocks on Mount Ida.

Grandfather Laomedon, who threatened to cut off the godly ears when their term was up, & they demanded payment.

Obviously, Apollo had little reason to love my city. & apples are his fruit.

Might Eris not have thrown the apple at the suggestion of Apollo. Who wanted to get back at Thetis for her denunciation. & at Hera, for the failure of her plot. & at Troy. Even if he pretended to be on our side, once the Greeks had set up their tents outside our walls.

Because he loved my brother Hector, supposedly. At least that was what he told Poseidon who couldn't understand why anyone would want to defend the memory of a humiliation.

Apollo did not save Hector from Achilles. But he carefully preserved Hector's dead flesh from rotting until my father was able to claim the body for burial.

The servants used to giggle, & whisper that Hector was Apollo's son. Which used to enrage me, as a child. Once I threatened to drag my nurse before my mother & make her ask my mother who Hector's father was, if they didn't stop giggling. They started cackling, & I hammered at my nurse with my fists. The thought of Hector being only one half my brother tormented me.

I began spying on my parents. Eavesdropping. Wondering if the continued grief I heard my father express over the death of his infant son   my second oldest brother Paris   was perhaps so deep & long lasting because Paris had actually been my father's first-born, with my mother. Hecabe's second son, but my father's first with her.

Later, the servants whispered the same thing about Troilus' birth. But I was older then, & had recently become prophetic. I was more interested in telling my mother that Troy would be safe forever if Troilus reached the age of twenty, than in asking who his   & Hector's Father was.

She would not have told me anyway. She probably would have looked distraught, & said that all children were gifts of the gods. Especially royal children, as I would no doubt find out for myself sooner or later. In spite of my childish insistence on remaining a virgin.

I did find out   a number of things   the day I turned down Apollo. My mother looked so incredulous when I told her   almost envious, I thought   that I was certain the servants had gossipped the truth. At least about Troilus' birth. Hecabe had obviously been in a similar position   twice, perhaps   but had given in.

19

Letting herself be mounted instead of giving herself. Perhaps it had not occurred to her that she could have said: No.

Perhaps it was occurring to her then that she could have said no also to my father. Instead of bearing him nineteen children: seven sons —one for each day of the week, & twelve daughters— one for each month of the year.

Meanwhile she kept urging me to run back to Thymbra at once, & apologize to Apollo with a sumptuous sacrifice. & if he deigned to reappear I was to embrace his feet.

He's after all a god, Cassandra: she kept saying. Wasn't I at all flattered by his divine desire for me?

I showed her my bruised knees & the blueing-browning imprints of his fingers at the base of my neck, & said that I'd have been more flattered if he had respected my wish not to be touched.

But he was a god . . . a god . . . : she kept repeating, wringing her hands. Was I afraid of getting pregnant & bearing a child? Was that why I wanted to remain a virgin?

I was sorry that I had told her. Expecting her to understand, & perhaps console me. She had never shown me much understanding before. & seemed to understand me less & less. We had never been particularly close. She was much closer to my older sisters, to Creusa & Laodice, & especially to Polyxena who looked a lot like her: dark-haired, with dark oval eyes under finely arched eyebrows. That did not

20

unlike mine   grow together above the
bridge of the nose.

I think I always made my mother feel ill
at ease. Before she began feeling ashamed of
me, & to blame my 'selfish' rejection of Apollo
for the misfortunes I was beginning to predict.
Which she may have foreseen herself, to
a certain extent. But didn't help me prevent
because, like many people, she couldn't
distinguish between her hunches & her fears.

She was my father's second wife, young
enough to have been his daughter. Which was
how she behaved toward him: docile, listening,
even after she became a grandmother.
—At least that was how their
relationship looked to me.
Perhaps she feared that my father would
divorce her, if she bothered him with glimpses
of a gloomy future. He was still reproaching her
for her dream of the flaming firebrand which
had led to what he believed to have been his son
Paris' death.
& he had divorced his first wife   Arisbe,
an outspoken woman, & the daughter of a
seer   after she bore him a son who interpreted
dreams.
My halfbrother Aesacus, who continued
to live in the palace after the divorce. It was
Aesacus who interpreted my mother's dream &
advised my father to have Paris killed at birth.
My father must have trusted him. More than

21

he trusted Helenus & me. Unless my father refused to listen to Helenus & me because he regretted having listened to Aesacus.

Arisbe promptly remarried. & was living   perhaps more happily   in a large white house that could be seen from the palace. From my mother's private chamber of polished stone. But of course she was no longer the Queen of Troy...

My mother had been raised in Locria, one of the last places to teach women the submissiveness she manifested. & tried to teach her daughters.

Locrian noblewomen were known for their independence. Which they maintained until Homeric times, almost half a millenium after Troy's fall. When they were forced to emigrate because of alleged 'pre-nuptial promiscuity & love affairs with slaves'...

Perhaps my mother had become submissive only after she married my father. Only after she dreamt the flaming firebrand that would destroy us all. Perhaps she was hoping to avoid the inevitable by slavish obedience. & lived like a slave, racked by daily fears.

Her main fear seems to have been displeasing. Her husband. The gods. Anyone who had any importance in her eyes. Odysseus... When there was nothing more to lose   after her worst fears had become reality   she suddenly let herself go, & changed into a bitch.

As I grew older, & began to link what was happening to what had happened in the past, I often wished grandfather Laomedon had paid the two punished gods for their year's work. & spared Troy the plague which Apollo sent in prompt retaliation. & Poseidon's sea monster, which vomited salt water over the fields outside the city gates, & drowned the crops.

Grandfather Laomedon may have thought that he had life-long credit with all the gods on Olympus after Zeus stole his nephew Ganymede. Whom Zeus' eagle had quietly picked up one fine windy morning, & carried off to the heavens, to become Zeus' personal cup bearer.

Perhaps he felt that the two immortal mares which Zeus sent down as compensation snow white & faster than a thunderstorm were an acknowledgment of divine debt.

I hesitate to think that my grandfather was just plain avaricious.

To the point of cheating. Not only Poseidon & Apollo, but also Heracles, who had offered to kill the sea monster in exchange for the two immortal mares.

For which my incorrigible grandfather substituted two ordinary mortal white nags, after the sea monster lay dead on the shore.

It cost him his life. Heracles slaughtered him, & all my uncles.

Which did, however, place my father Priam on the throne. Grandfather's only surviving son. Only a boy at the time, named Podares. My father became Priam —which means: redeemed— when my aunt Hesione bought back his freedom with her golden veil.

My aunt herself was taken as booty to Greece by Telamon, Heracles' friend & ally, who had fallen in love with her, & to whom she was allotted as his share of the spoils.

As a child I often heard my father speak about his beautiful older sister. Swearing that he would bring her back to Troy. By force, if need be.

One day we received word that she had walked out on Telamon   without the young son she had born him   & had disappeared. She had swum all the way across the Cretan Sea, to Miletus.

I used to have many childish phantasies about my beautiful aunt who loved things made of gold, & refused to remain a conqueror's loot. Even though Telamon adored her, supposedly. & had made her his lawful wife: according to my mother. According to my father: he had not.

Little did I know then   a still unprophetic child of five or six   that my fate would be precisely that. Only worse. The man who claimed me as his loot was married. To an embittered wife who was oldfashioned enough to think that she had rights. &, though adulterous herself, tried to enforce her rights: with a double-bladed ax.

I was the victim of both social orders: of Apollo's waxing patriarchy, & of Clytemnestra's last spasms of outraged matriarchy. My father Priam probably would have said: that I had asked for it. That no society could be expected to tolerate an individual who insisted on telling the truth.

On *yelling* the truth: my father probably would have said.

—Clytemnestra's son Orestes was the first man to be acquitted of matricide.

During the trial in Athens, Appollo said in Orestes' defense that: the mother was the unimportant parent. That a woman was no more than a passive furrow into which the man cast his seed. His definition became the epitaph of women's dignity throughout the world.

I'm sorry to say that my protectress Athena agreed with Apollo. But then, Athena had been born without a mother. She had been Zeus' brainchild, burst forth from her father's head.

I remember teasing Agamemnon during the crossing to Mycenae. Asking if he thought that he now *owned* my shoulders. Which he kept hugging.

& what about the twins? Did he think they were loot, like their mother? Or conquerors, like their father? Or half and half:

was Pelops the loot, & Teledamus the conqueror; or the other way round? Or were they maybe taking turns?

He hugged me again   more closely to him   & said that: he would always be my slave.

He had been hugging me an awful lot, since we shipped out from Troy. From what was left of it. It seemed as though he couldn't keep his hands off me.

The sardonic glee which I had acquired during the holocaust—   &   during the tempestuous crossing; when Agamemnon thought that I was 'giddy with negativity' made me play with the notion that the account of Ajax raping me at the foot of Athena's statue, whose outraged owl eyes had turned aside when I focused on them, trying to draw the image down, to make it topple forward & crush the Locrian's humping rump; & me beneath it   was stimulating Agamemnon's desire for me. & that his imagination was filling in additional details. With himself in the Locrian's position. Or rather   more in keeping with his character   in the position of the statue. That would, however, have looked on.

Agamemnon had always struck me as a spectator. Who thought that he was directing whatever he was watching. Of course I hadn't known him when he was a young man.

Actually he was probably hugging me so much to reassure himself by reassuring me that: everything was going to be all right. He couldn't wait to 'straighten things out' with Clytemnestra.

Either he had forgotten how adamant he had always told me Clytemnestra was. Or else he thought that having a lover had mellowed her. & weakened her unforgiving infallibility.

I knew otherwise, of course. But I had given up warning him. He was a king; he missed his throne. & I had had enough. Unlike Agamemnon, I had come to see death as a relief.

Which it may be. For less rebellious, blinder mortals. Who exit more gently   with their head on   from a less blatant life.

Followers of varying religions who pass through the underworld in quest of new forms of existence, & stop at the name: Cassandra some to proselytize, some to console; most of them to ask if I can still predict the future, & if so, what future I foresee for them   have said to me that a violent death may freeze the spirit. Sometimes for several millennia.

For several centuries my rebel spirit stood petrified in a shrine outside Mycenae. Where girls who wanted to rid themselves of an unwelcome suitor would come & bring offerings & embrace my statue.

If some of my contemporaries   men & women   found me foolish for turning down a god   —forfeiting my chance of bearing an immortal baby—   I became totally incomprehensible to men & women of later

times, who had made Apollo into THE IDEAL
MAN. The embodiment of human progress &
enlightenment. I had incomprehensibly
spurned the dawning light, & clung to
reactionary notions, miring my life in darkness.

But I was not the only woman of
antiquity who refused to be 'chosen'. Which
was becoming the fashionable euphemism for
being raped while I was still alive.

The nymph Daphne had herself changed
into a laurel, to extricate herself from Apollo's
embrace. & Castilia of Delphi, a mortal like me,
threw herself down a well to get away from
him.

Another nymph, Sinope, rejected Zeus
himself. She asked to be granted a wish   —as
was the custom— before she complied with
his. & when Zeus did, she wished to remain a
virgin.

Apparently she lived happily ever after.
Zeus was less vindictive than Apollo. At least
toward women. He loved, when he made love.
He wasn't competing, or getting even.

—Except with Hera, on occasion. As I
have said: their marriage was the battleground
on which the sexes began their fight for
supremacy. But women had as yet not lost out.
They were still able to grant or to withhold
their consent.

Zeus often used trickery to obtain it. But
consent was important to him. He belonged to
the pre-Apollonian age to which I was allegedly
clinging. Which was still accustomed to women

having a mind of their own. To women having
a mind.

Apollo also granted wishes. But he was
the deceiver more often than the deceived. I'm
not just thinking of what he did to me. But of
the far less ambiguous case of the unfortunate
sybil of Cumae, to whom he gave as many years
of life as grains of sand or grains of dust
but withheld the customarily associated
gift of youth. The miserable woman ended
up hanging inside an amphora, shrivelled,
toothless, & bald, begging to die. She
may still be hanging inside the amphora;
I never heard of her release.

The many contradictory legends which
continue to circulate about me usually agree
that I was 'favored' by Apollo.

That he courted me   —which he did;
when I was 16—   & gave me the gift of
prophecy   —which he did *not*; at least not
directly—in exchange for my promised consent.

That I accepted his gift deceitfully, since I
had no intention of keeping my promise. & that
he was amply justified when he spat into my
mouth & made me unbelievable. I got what I
deserved. My fate was fair.

Since the advent of 'psychology',
invented by a grim-bearded patriarch
disconcertingly named 'Joy', who raided our
myths & legends for labels to affix to modern
mortal behavior patterns, everything we used

to do has become 'symbolic' of something else.
Thus it has been suggested that Apollo's
spitting kiss was symbolic of my sexual union
with the god. Which is to have been the
prerequisite for acquiring my oracular powers.

Just as blindness   the act of blinding   is
to have been symbolic of castration, the alleged
prerequisite for male seers.

The celibacy of priests & monks, during
later centuries, as well as the weddingband
worn by nuns, are alleged hangovers from such
sexual rites that were allegedly the custom
during & before my time.

I don't object to these theories, as long as
they're not applied to me. They can't be applied
to me, since Apollo had not given me my
oracular powers, but was, on the contrary,
taking them away from me when he kissed me.

The thought of him mounting
me   symbolically or otherwise   is as degrading
to me as the memory of Ajax on top of my
flailing body during the final hours of Troy's
doom.

It is not true that I deceived Apollo. I
never played coy with him, or made him any
promises. I was a tomboy, at 16. I wouldn't
have known how to flirt if I had wanted to. I
gave him no grounds whatsoever to assume
that I would yield to his desire.

Which disgusted me, it was so
imperative.

& perhaps faked. A ruse. Perhaps Apollo never desired me, but couldn't think of any other means than courting me to get close enough to my mouth to invalidate my prophetic gift.

—Which he had NOT given to me. Which his serpents gave to me   & to my twin brother Helenus; on our 7th birthday—.

I've tried in vain to remember the expression on Apollo's face   if he seemed to be laughing at me when he proclaimed that my 'superb ankles & touchingly small feet were trampling on his divine heart'.

Agamemnon said more or less the same thing. But he kissed my toes   one by one while he said it. Apollo had me pinned against his altar, in Thymbra, his fingers hard around my throat. Before he forced his tongue into my mouth. After he had tripped me, after chasing me around his altar nine times.

I was certainly not the only mortal who became the target of Apollo's revenge. But the form of his revenge is singularly ambiguous, in my case. Why would he have prevented me from being heard   & believed   when he was allegedly on the side of Troy. Which could have been saved, if I had been heard & believed.

—Unless his true ambition was not to save Troy   a doomed civilization that had as yet no laws for punishing non-submissive women   but to go down in history as the noble defender of a once-great people. About whom history becomes notoriously sentimental, once the greatness has collapsed.

I was born on the cusp between the right side & the wrong side of time, having been born a woman in my era; in my city.

Perhaps Troy was slowly sliding from the right side to the wrong side. From a time of commerce to a renaissance of conquests. Which the renegade seer Calchas had seen when he switched sides, & betrayed us to the Greeks at the very beginning of the hostilities.

Which my twin brother Helenus also saw; a number of years later. When Troy landslid to the wrong side, as far as he was concerned, when my father persuaded Helen to marry our other brother, Deiphobus, after Paris' death.

I used to think that the people of Troy were celebrating Helenus' & my birthday, when they swarmed out to Thymbra on the 21st day of June. To celebrate the summer solstice with sacrifices & picnics & dancing, late into the windy moonlit night.

I used to love our birthdays. Especially our 7th birthday, which stood out in my memory as the most radiant day of my life, during most of the nine years that followed.

Helenus & I had been given our first cup of wine to share. He'd drunk most of it, & turned green.

Helenus always had a sensitive stomach,
& headaches. He was a pale sickly boy whom
our nurse used to torture with potions &
enemas. He didn't want her to stick her sandy
fingers down his throat, & hid behind a column
in the temple until she'd gone outside with the
others. When he felt better we played
sacrificing each other behind Apollo's altar.

Where both of us must have fallen
asleep. Because that was where our nurse
found us, later that afternoon. Curled up inside
a nest of serpents that were licking our eyes &
ears.

I can still see the nurse's wine-flushed
face, her wide open screaming mouth. —Her.
teeth were as brown as her eyes.— Although
afterwards she always denied that she had
screamed. Waking us up; scaring the serpents
away. She always insisted that she had known
right away that the serpents weren't doing us
any harm. That they were making us
prophetic.

I used to think that the gift of prophecy
was the most wonderful birthday present I
could have wished for.

From that day on Helenus & I began
predicting minor household events. The
weather, mainly.

Once, my mother stopped beating one of
the slaves when I said that the woman was
innocent. That it was my baby brother Troilus
who had tottered against the new   now

33

broken   amphora which depicted the Palladium
falling from heaven, into the camp of my
greatgrandfather Ilus, who built the city of
Troy around it.

The Palladium was a legless wooden
statue of a young girl, holding a spear in her
raised right hand. Athena herself had carved it,
in memory of her playmate Pallas whom she
had accidentally run through, still during her
divine adolescence, when the two girls had been
playing war on Olympus. One day Zeus had
tripped over it, & thrown it out.

No enemy could take the city in which
the Palladium stood. My contemporaries used
to call it: the luck of Troy. —Which Odysseus
stole; or rather: has been 'credited' with
stealing.— Copies of it are still being shown in
a number of places, which all claim that their
statue is the original.

I was believable   even to my mother
between 7 & 16, before Apollo noticed me.

Helenus remained believable for as long
as he lived. To a ripe old age; which often
seems to be the case of sickly children. If not of
traitors.

Even so, my father didn't listen to
Helenus either when both of us begged him to
kill our brother Paris, when Paris reappeared in
Troy.

—I did *not* try to kill Paris myself. With
an ax. In spite of pictures of me that are still in

existence on shards of crockery, & mural
fragments   of what legend has made me out to
have been: wild-haired, crazy-eyed, raising the
ax which a gently frowning Aphrodite wrestles
from my fist.

My eyes may have looked strange at
times. As I have said: they rolled back,
supposedly, when I fell into a trance. But my
blond curly hair was always neatly braided,
intertwined with purple ribbons. It came
undone only when Clytemnestra cut through
the end of the braid when she cut off my head.

I've always felt a wry admiration for
Paris' uninhibited judgment, crowning the least
harmful   & therefore the least useful   of the
three goddesses.

Of course he may have thought at the
time that a shepherd's insignificance gave him
the freedom to be truthful. He couldn't know
that his personal fate was going to implicate an
entire city.

Or else he may have thought that
women could do no harm to a man such as he.
Even when they were   rejected   godesses.
He had as yet not rejected the fountain
nymph Oenone who had chosen him
as her lover. He was young & beautiful, & the
world was his arena.

At that point in his life the shepherd
Alexander was mainly interested in organizing
bullfights.

Paris later claimed that he had suggested
cutting the apple up into three equal sections, &
awarding each goddess a third. But that
Hermes who had flown the apple down to him
on Mount Ida had slapped the knife from his
hand & told him not to play games with Zeus'
orders. Hermes' face had looked fierce, almost
ugly, without his habitual smile.

It was to accompany his prize bull that
Alexander/Paris came to Troy.
Where he couldn't resist competing in the
funeral games my father was holding in his
memory. In memory of the twenty-fourth
birthday of his second son, who was supposed
to have died a few hours after his birth, exposed
to the wild animals & the elements of Mount
Ida. By one of my father's herdsmen who had,
however, taken the royal baby home & raised it
as a son of his own.

—Paris preferred the servants' version of
his story which began circulating soon after his
return: He had been adopted & nursed by a
female bear. & had been found playfully
wrestling with a cub, at an older age   at 5 or 6
or 7   by my father's herdsman, who ... etc. ...

Helenus & I watched the eager young
shepherd win the wrestling match against
Hector   with bearlike determination rather
than with technique   & the footrace against
Deiphobus, flying ahead of Deiphobus like a

pursued cattle thief, & thought we were
watching a wrestling, racing firebrand. That
was going to burn Troy to the ground.

We knew instantly who the shepherd
was, & rushed to tell Priam.

Who believed us enough to reclaim the
shepherd as his much-mourned son.

He was overjoyed that the gods were
giving Paris back. As a birthday present to the
father, obviously, whose repentant grief had
moved them. He was not going to 'insult their
generosity' by committing the murder a second
time. He'd rather lose Troy than this beautiful
courageous god-given son: he said to us,
struggling to his gout-swollen feet. Pushing us
out of his way.

Helenus said that he would lose Paris
anyway. & other courageous sons besides. As
well as Troy.

I said nothing. My mother was stepping
on my left foot. Painfully hard.

You have the wrong attitude, Cassandra,
she hissed into my ear. You're attracting
disaster, with your predictions.

My father grabbed her arm. Together
they stumbled down into the stadium.

Helenus & I ran after them. I was
limping slightly. I felt like one of the Erinnyes,
except for my neater hair. Once again I
wondered if Paris was my father's first-born,
with my mother. If Hector was Apollo's son.

If we had kept quiet, Hector &
Deiphobus would probably have killed the

young herdsman, whose blunt unskilled victories had humiliated them. They had Paris cornered at one of the stadium exits & were tickling his throat with their swords when my parents fluttered down upon them.

My mother threw herself against the bewildered herdsman's sweaty chest, sobbing: My baby   my baby   my baby...

Helenus looked at them, & then at me, with raised eyebrows. He shrugged, & walked away.

My father was giving orders for a banquet.

Paris' striking good looks & easy charm increased my prejudice against him. He was better built than Hector, with a brow nobler than Troilus', but smoother, caressable like the face of a young lion. & he was in every way as entertaining as Deiphobus.

A mortal Apollo: I thought, disgusted.

He seemed to know exactly how to say what to everyone of us. Spontaneously, without any apparent attempt at flattery. Yet, all of us were flattered. Even Andromache looked animated when he talked with her.

With me, he seemed mainly to be listening.

I told myself that he was working hard at ingratiating himself all around. To hush the echo of the ugly oracle that had preceded his birth. Which his return had revived. Whispered repetitions of my mother's

nightmare made the streets & the servants'
quarters sound like a summernight filled with
cicadas.

But when I spoke with him, his concern
for Troy's fate felt so sincere to me that I
thought he could perhaps be persuaded to go
back to bucolic anonymity. To the fountain
nymph Oenone whom he said he missed.

& glowingly described. She was
wise   he told me   & could heal wounds &
illnesses. But she was also exquisitely beautiful.
With a finely curved nose, & blond curly hair,
small round breasts, & grey oblong eyes under a
single eyebrow. But what he liked best about
her   he said   were her tiny feet & lovely
ankles.

He was describing me to myself in the
most flattering terms possible. I refused to be
bribed, & walked away.

But when I overheard him later telling
Deiphobus how much I reminded him of his
wise beautiful Oenone   asking Deiphobus how
many women he had met who were gifted with
a special knowledge & looked like adorable
young boys   I felt once more impressed with
his sincerity.

I started wandering through the palace,
looking for Hector. I wanted Hector to talk to
Paris at once, to talk him into disappearing
again before he charmed all Trojans into
agreeing with my father: that they would
rather lose their city than their newly found
prince.

I didn't see Hector anywhere &
finally   reluctantly   went to his apartments.
        Andromache received me with one of her
patient smiles that always seemed to say: Yes,
dear? Just what seems to be the matter this
time?
        Hector was lying down. She wasn't
going to disturb him.
        She made me drink a cup of goat's
buttermilk, which was supposed to be good for
my nerves. We had one of our usual pointless
conversations, which came alive briefly when I
mused about the peculiar partiality of parents
who seemed to prefer a returned stranger to
their other sons who had stayed at home.
        Andromache was a wholesome woman
with little imagination. &, so far as I could tell,
no sense of humor. Totally wrapped up in
being 'Hector's wife'. She believed that the
gods loved those who lived right, the way
Hector & she were living. If I had reminded her
of my mother's dream, & told her that Helenus
& I both had seen the same flaming firebrand
wrestle with her Hector in the stadium that
morning, she probably would have made me
drink another cup of buttermilk, & said that a
good husband was the best cure for
superstitious fears. She was yawning.

        I looked at this earnest well-meaning
woman who was standing like a guard outside
my brother's bedchamber. Who refused to let
me speak to him, when I had spoken to him

every day of my life   & he to me   until he
married her.

Why had this woman become the wife of
my favorite brother? Whom I thought I had
known so well. Whom I had always understood
before.

The hero of my childhood. Who had
taught me how to hold & throw a spear   & a
discus   & to ride a horse against the wind.
Behind the disapproving back of my mother
who wanted her daughters to grow into
modern desirable women, unencumbered by
oldfashioned amazon skills.

My teacher-protector-accomplice, who
laughed away the games I lost. & asked me
every day if it was all right to go out or if it was
going to rain, after I first became prophetic.

But hadn't asked me if it was going to
rain, the day he went out to marry
Andromache.

A woman who agreed with my mother
that I was 'not normal'. For having turned down
a god, I imagine. Although I knew that she
would have screamed for Hector until her voice
gave out, if anyone   immortal or mortal   had
tried to come near enough to compliment her
on her eyelids.

—Which were beautiful, like dew-
polished petals, Hector had told me after he
first met her.

She thought   & said   that I was jealous
of her. & perhaps I was. Not because I had 'an
abnormal attachment to my brother', as she said

to my mother   & to Polyxena who told me
but because she had made it impossible for
me to talk with Hector.

Even on the rare occasions when Hector
& I happened to be together somewhere where
she was not, I could no longer talk with him.
We had nothing more to say to each other, &
would stand facing each other with sheepish
smiles, exchanging banalities. It was as though
Andromache had absorbed all his former
interests. Except, perhaps, the welfare of Troy.
In which her welfare was included.

Suddenly her yawning face became a
hideous grimace. I saw her open mouth bite
into freshly dug earth; her fingers clawing at
her hair.

Andromache! I gasped.

She patted my arm, hiding another yawn
in a broad patient smile. Good night...

Fate was on its way. It was arrogant of
me to think that I could deflect it from its
course.

I couldn't help admiring its patience.

& the seeming casualness of its timing:
The next morning Menelaus arrived from
Delphi.

He was a soft-spoken soft-bearded
baldman, better known as the husband of Helen
than as Sparta's king. A position he had
acquired by marrying Helen.

On the surface, his visit looked totally

unrelated to anything that might concern my
city. A plague was besieging Sparta. Menelaus
had gone to consult the Delphic oracle to find
out how the plague could be stopped. He had
been advised to offer heroic sacrifices to
Prometheus' sons. Their tombs happened to be
in Troy.

But Menelaus instantly befriended my
brother Paris. Who wined & dined him lavishly.
& may sincerely have returned Menelaus'
friendship, although the two men seemed to
have very little in common. Except for Helen,
but Helen had as yet not entered the scene. She
had not accompanied her husband.

The people of Troy were keenly
disappointed not to see Zeus' fabled daughter.
Whose skin was said to be the same translucent
white as the divine swan egg from which her
mother Leda had hatched her.

—Together with her twin brother Pollux.
Clytemnestra & Castor had crawled from a
second   mortal; off-white   egg.

There was much speculation why Helen
had chosen Menelaus, over hundreds of at least
equally plausible suitors.

—The poorest & least plausible among
them had been Odysseus. Whose irrelevant
suggestion that all the assembled princes pledge
to defend the man of Helen's ultimate choice
earned him the hand of Helen's cousin
Penelope. Only the gods knew at the moment

of the oath that the most powerful princes in Greece who were standing in Sparta's market place   on the bloody chunks of a dismembered horse   were pledging to make war on Troy. —

For weeks I heard my sisters ask my mother if Helen had married Menelaus because he was the brother of Agamemnon. & Agamemnon was married to Helen's sister Clytemnestra. Two sisters marrying two brothers. If it had perhaps amused Helen to become her own sister-in-law...

& I overheard my mother asking our old nurse if she remembered a certain rumor that had gone around some fifteen to twenty years before. Suggesting that Agamemnon was the uncle rather than the father of Iphigeneia. Whom Helen's sister Clytemnestra was raising as her own daughter, but who was perhaps Helen's daughter. Whom Helen had perhaps borne when she was fourteen, or thirteen, or perhaps younger, if the certain rumor was true. If Theseus had abducted Helen & married her, when she was fourteen or thirteen or twelve... When she had not stayed with Theseus, but had gone to stay with her sister in Mycenae until she was in shape to go home again...

I didn't hear anyone suggest that Helen might have preferred Menelaus to the hundreds of   perhaps hairy, strong-voiced   suitors. That she might have loved him.

Not any more than I heard anyone doubt that Helen had fallen in love with my brother

Paris, when Paris brought Helen to Troy.

Which I myself came to doubt only years
later. After Paris had been killed, & she looked
just as content to be married to my other
brother, Deiphobus. When I began to wonder if
Helen was capable of falling in love.

& when I saw her walk down to the
Greek ships, on Menelaus' arm once again, after
it was all over, after Deiphobus had just been
slaughtered, lying next to her on their bed, & I
saw that she was smiling, on Menelaus' arm, I
stared at her in awe.

She waved to me as I stood frozen,
staring after her. Asking myself if this woman
whom I had befriended was a monster of
indifference. Who had no feelings except for
her own safety & comfort.

—Although I had seen her take beggars
home with her. Washing their feet, & giving
them food . . .

Because she felt that living in poverty
was a worse fate than being murdered?

Or did this woman possess a knowledge
that was deeper than mine? & useful, unlike
mine? An understanding of life that allowed
her to smile like the moon?

Paris had been persuading my father to
give him a fleet, & let him leave with his new
friend Menelaus.

He wanted to go on an expedition, &
bring back my aunt Hesione. At least that was

what he said to my father. Helenus & I knew whom Paris would end up bringing back to Troy, & we protested.

It made my mother violently angry. With me. What on earth is the matter with you, Cassandra! she scolded. First Paris wasn't to be allowed inside our city gates, & now you don't want him to leave. Why don't you get married, & live your own life for a change!

When Helenus asked her if she had forgotten her dream, she gestured as though to slap my face.

It was Paris who caught her hand. Cassandra means well, Mother, he said, stroking her fingers. & she's probably right. She sees further than the rest of us.

I said Helenus saw just as far. & our mother could see ahead too, if only she'd have the courage to look.

Please don't leave: I begged him.

He looked as though he wanted to cry. Apparently the expression on my face was the same as Oenone's when she, too, had asked him not to go.

I do love her. Sincerely, he said sadly. I love Troy. I love you all. One half of me longs to stay, but the other half doesn't want to let down Aphrodite.

I said that I had turned down the great Apollo . . .

Unfortunately, for all of us, my mother sighed.

I'd been getting more impossible every

day, since that day, she said to Paris, looping
her arm through his, drawing him a few steps
away. The less attention one paid to me, the
better off one was, I heard her whisper. I was
not a normal woman . . .

I felt that my mother disliked me, & it
made me suffer. She seemed to derive a
righteous satisfaction from humiliating me. As
though she wanted to punish me for being
different from herself, & my other sisters.

Which I was, of course. I shared none of
their tastes or values. Prestige, which meant
much to them, offended me when I looked at
the men who were heroes in their eyes.

Perhaps one other reason for giving
myself to Agamemnon   a reason I'm still
embarrassed to admit, because it shows how
suffering mollified my principles   was to regain
my mother's esteem. It did improve our
relationship on the surface, but it didn't make
us become close. & it helped neither her nor me
to escape the final catastrophe. Besides, it had
probably been preordained.

Agamemnon was certain that our coming
together had been arranged by the gods. Who
favored him, & wanted to see him happy.

I don't want to sound pretentious, but I
really think that he was happy with me.
Disarmingly; in spite of a war of which he
disapproved. Which he had vainly tried to
prevent. & vainly continued to try to bring to a
stop. In which he had been forced to play a

leading role.

He called it: the Phantom War. Which both armies were fighting over the illusion that their leaders were fighting over Helen. Whose private life had little to do with Greek access to the Hellespont. An agreement controlling the trade routes might have been reached less expensively by negotiation. Before the war dispensed with the need for an agreement, by destroying the trade.

It amuses me to think that later legends borrowed Agamemnon's 'phantom war' in their attempt to clean up Helen's morals for patriarchal consumption when they suggest that the 'real' Helen not only resisted Paris' advances in Sparta, but that she managed to get away from him in Egypt. & that the plight of her domestic virtue moved either Hera   or Zeus   or Aphrodite (Aphrodite indeed)   to slip a dummy Helen into the bed of my lascivious brother. Which he triumphantly brought home to Troy, while the real Helen continued to live in Egypt, incognita, in virtuous seclusion.

& neither Paris   nor my adoring father   nor any of us   noticed anything, during the many long years the dummy lived among us.

Except my brother Hector. The only Trojan whom legend honors as a hero, & places just a step or two below Achilles. (Because he was Apollo's son? But so was Troilus.)

Hector alone saw through the divinely

48

virtuous ruse. That's why he had so little use for the Helen all of Troy adored. Hector knew all along that the war was being fought over a phantom, as Agamemnon had said . . .

I asked Agamemnon once if the rumor was true, about Helen & Theseus. Out of curiosity, I guess. Although curiosity was not one of my vices. I usually felt that I knew more than was good for me.

I also knew that Agamemnon was extremely touchy on the subject of Iphigeneia. I carefully avoided mentioning her.

He looked at me searchingly before he finally said that he knew few men who had not wanted to marry Helen at one time or another. But if I was insinuating that he had sacrificed his niece to obtain clement sailing weather, he wanted me to know that it would never occur to him to sacrifice a woman. Did I really think he was a modern barbarian? He had sacrificed a goat, that day at Aulis. He had told Clytemnestra the truth when he sent for Iphigeneia to come to Aulis: To marry her to Achilles.

Yach: I grimaced. I couldn't tell which was worse, being sacrificed, or marrying Achilles.

He beamed. It pleased him that I had no use for Achilles. Or for Odysseus. Or even for Apollo. It added a gloss of uniqueness to his image of himself as my lover. He didn't know that I would have had no use for him either,

had he still been the conquering hero who
married Clytemnestra by force, after murdering
her first husband, & the infant son at her
breast.

Clytemnestra had many reasons   besides
my arrival under her roof; with the twins, my
sons by her husband   for wishing to put an end
to Agamemnon. Whether he had sacrificed her
daughter, or her niece. Or a goat.

It is only too well known   &
unfortunately true   that Paris sailed with
Menelaus to Sparta. Directly & rapidly, with
the most auspicious of breezes, courtesy of
Aphrodite. My aunt Hesione was forgotten
even as a pretext.

For nine days Menelaus feasted him.
Giving his wife ample time to fall in love with
Paris. —If Helen was capable of falling in
love.— Paris had been in love with the prospect
of falling in love with Helen   with the image of
Helen & himself together, as a couple   since
the day Aphrodite promised her to him in
exchange for Eris' apple.

I have sometimes wondered whatever
happened to that apple. Wishing that it had
been good & green, if Aphrodite ate it after she
won it. That it had given her an immortal
bellyache. But it was probably left to rot in
some corner of Olympus, while we dumb mortals
down below perpetuated the fight over it,
fertilizing the soil for future appletrees   &

future applemen   with our predestined flesh &
blood. Our bleeding-hero worship.

On the morning of the tenth day
Menelaus had to leave for Crete, to attend the
funeral of his grandfather Catreus. Paris &
Helen eloped that same evening.
...Taking with them every movable
palace treasure. All the gold from Apollo's
temple outside the gates of Sparta. & several
servants. Only Helen's eight-year-old daughter
Hermione was left behind.
Many accounts have accused Helen &
Paris of robbing Menelaus 'shamelessly'. &
have given robbery as the main reason for the
war against my city.
—Which was a trade war. Troy
controlled the Black Sea trade routes.
The later the accounts, the greater care
they take to forget   or to obliterate   that
Sparta was still matrilinear at Helen's & my
time, even if she was ruled by kings. Queen
Helen owned the treasures she took away with
her. She had inherited them.
& if she left Hermione behind   but not
her two-year-old son Pleisthenes   it was not, as
has been held against her, because she was an
ill-loving biased mother.
How can anyone believe that the most
famous woman of her time   the most beautiful
& lastingly youthful; whom most men desired
& most women tried to imitate   had so
slavishly fallen under my brother's spell that

51

she abandoned a helpless little girl to the wrath of a betrayed husband, because she allegedly 'feared eventual competition from a growing daughter'! When, in actuality, she was leaving the heiress to the Spartan throne. Which she herself was renouncing, by her departure.

For love of an increasingly unworthy adventurer: according to the same accounts. Which do not hesitate to turn an initially intrepid pursuer of (cattle) thieves into a thief & a coward, suddenly, after his 'netting' of Helen.

Whom they either change into a phantom   so as not to tax their wish-dreaming readers' hypocrisy: finding themselves desiring an adulterous woman   or else portray as a hand-wringing wife who wanders about the streets of Troy plagued by guilt & remorse, deploring her weakness to anyone who will listen.

But Helen   —& I—   lived before the introduction of the double standard. When wives were still known to take lovers. Although few went as far as giving up their property in the process.

Penelope, the Spartan Duck, whom legend has erected as a monument of conjugal fidelity, doing therapy on her loom, slept with every one of the quarrelling suitors   —which was why they were quarrelling—   until Odysseus finally returned.

Helen was merely franker   & therefore perhaps more reckless   than other women of our time. Perhaps she felt more secure than other women, in her life-long youthfulness & beauty, which was considered to be the greatest asset of any person, female & male, in our society.

The gods knew what they were doing when they brought Helen & Paris together to trigger the war that was to rebalance life on earth. Helen & Paris were the 'ideal couple'. An icon, from which the less beautiful rest of humanity expected its redemption.

My defense of Helen may surprise   my friendship with her surprised everyone, including myself   after all the fuss I had made to keep Paris away from her. & Helen away from Troy.

I had even written to Paris in Sparta, suggesting that they go off together somewhere   to Egypt perhaps; anywhere but Troy   & that he take her back to her husband when they felt they had fulfilled Aphrodite's promise to them both.

But I refused then   & I still refuse   to blame the tool, & worship the manipulator.

Paris & Helen did stop off in Egypt, as I had suggested. But a fling was not what the gods intended. The ideal couple must love unto death, with an undying passion.

That must, however, not manifest outwardly beyond a tender kiss, & longing looks. The ideal couple must know exactly what it wants, & stick with it.

One windy fall morning they landed in Troy.

My parents received Helen with open arms. Especially my mother, who displayed ostentatious joy. Darting warning glances in my direction as she took Helen by one reputedly fair white hand & led her in triumph to the apartments my father had prepared for the newsmaking newlyweds. In the east wing of the palace, across from Hector's & Andromache's apartments.

My father enjoyed having his sons live & breed around him. It made him feel like a radiant sun
—the slowly rising masculine source of life. That used to be the source of death, in moon-ruled matriarchies. Although I have discovered that there are cultures   in particular to the northwest of us   that speak of the sun as female, & of the moon as male...

My father vowed never NEVER to let Helen go. Back to Menelaus. The banquet he gave in her honor lasted a full month, from one new moon to the next. Troy went mad over Helen.
—Except my brother Hector who kept referring to her as 'the adulterous Spartan Queen'. It made Andromache walk around like a contented cow, her pregnant stomach preceding her beatific smile.

Helen's friendship came as a pleasant surprise. A relief from the cautious mildness with which my family had been treating me since the day Paris left with Menelaus. When I had been seized by a vision while I was standing at the dock, looking after their departing ships.

Helenus later told me that I had suddenly flung myself into the shallow water at the shore, & had lain flailing on the wet rocks, frothing at the mouth, fighting off an invisible attacker. Tearing the clothes from my body. Screaming that I was being raped.

It was the first & only time that a vision made me lose consciousness.

I was lying in my room when I came to, wrapped in a servant's tunic. There were bruises on my knees & on my thighs; & on my neck. Our old nurse was putting damp fennel leaves on them with furtive fingers. I looked up into the moon-crater landscape that was her face. She averted her eyes.

Later that evening Helenus came to my room & told me what had happened. He had seen in full what I had glimpsed before I blanked out. He probably wouldn't have remained conscious either if he had seen himself being raped: he said consolingly.

He was trying to be kind. From that day on, the rest of the household looked at me as though I had been afflicted with a disgraceful disease. That might be catching if one came too close.

After a while Helenus also began staying away.

I had expected Helen to avoid me like the

others. Perhaps more so. She had every reason
to bear me a grudge if she knew how
vehemently I had protested against her coming
to Troy. Paris had probably shown her my
letter.

I had planned to call on her in her new
apartments, formally, a day or two after she
settled in.

I had prepared what I was going to say to
her. That I had nothing against her as a person.
That I was merely trying to prevent the
catastrophe I had seen her trigger in a number
of visions I had had.

In one   which kept recurring   she was
igniting the firebrand that was to burn down
our city. In another, which I had had only once
so far & hoped not to have again because it was
so horrible, she was holding my brother
Deiphobus' genitals cupped in her fair white
hands, offering them to Menelaus like a bloody
bouquet.

It was she who came to call on me   not
at all formally   almost immediately after her
arrival. I can still see her standing between the
two columns at the entrance to my room, still in
her travel clothes, holding a tailless cat which
she had brought with her from Egypt where
these animals were sacred   especially those
born without a tail   & were thought to bring
luck to their owner for the fifteen or twenty
years that was their lifespan.

She was smiling. Stretching one hand
toward me, under the cat's tailless rear, saying

that she hoped we would be friends.

We did become friends. & it became a protection for me. It was because of how it would look to Helen that my father didn't follow up on any of his repeated threats: to have me locked up if I didn't keep quiet.

Nonetheless, I kept urging her to leave Troy the sooner the better before she became the pretext for a war.

She kept assuring me that she would leave although she would hate to walk out on the welcome we all had given her; she would hate to disappoint my father Priam before it came to 'that'.

Which she doubted. It would be too stupid. Did I really believe that politics were still being conducted on that primitive a level. In our day & age. Surely we had reached the age of negotiation.

I said: Stupidity was timeless. It was immortal & would outlive us all. Even my friend Helen of the Fair Hands.

Whom I saw living to a serene old age: I told her.

Sometimes I almost believed that she would leave. & felt that I would miss her.

I thought she understood me. She had not been in the least surprised or critical that I had refused Apollo. Perhaps she shared my aversion for conquering heroes. Whom she certainly didn't need to improve her social position. It was she who added glamour to her men. Even to Theseus, with whom rumor had perhaps linked her mainly to intensify *his* glory.

I never asked Helen about Theseus. She didn't invite personal questions. She rarely talked about herself, about what had happened to her in the past.

That she seemed to understand me, & to like me nonetheless, restored some of my self-confidence.

Which was far less solid than it may look in retrospect. Doubts tormented me as much as my visions. Perhaps I was a sick hysterical girl whose 'negative outlook on life' was due to 'sexual difficulties', as my mother had said after my convulsions on the shore. Apologizing to my father for having borne him an embarrassing daughter.

It was lonely knowing what no one wanted to know.

Perhaps making everyone feel understood was Helen's secret:

My parents called her their 'most considerate daughter'.

Paris felt that Helen respected him for the moral integrity behind his charm. Whereas Oenone had loved him as a pet.

Deiphobus thought that she admired his courage. Which made him face danger open-eyed, unlike most other men who usually lacked his intelligence & imagination, & were blindly courageous, by reflex.

& Helenus, who lived in a loneliness
similar to mine, inmidst our family   who had
been lonely longer than I, since he had often
been excluded from our games when he was a
boy, because of his sensitive stomach; who had
not had Hector as his childhood teacher &
friend   Helenus felt that Helen was the cure of
all his ills. That Helen & Helenus   rather than
Helen & Paris   had been meant to form the
ideal couple.

He desperately wanted to marry her,
after Paris' death, & walked out on Troy when
my father convinced Helen to marry his
other   healthier   son Deiphobus.

It was because of Helen that Helenus
betrayed the secrets of Troy's safety to the
Greeks.

& probably suggested the ruse of the
wooden horse. In which I always thought I
recognized the imprint of my brother's mind. It
wouldn't be the first time that Odysseus took
credit for another man's idea, after it succeeded.
Or that others gave him the credit for it,
amplifying his hero reputation with the glorious
deeds of the less heroic.

Perhaps my friend Helen was
everybody's friend. Because no one was
important enough to her to bother being
unfriendly, perhaps. Perhaps I was as self-
involved as everybody else when I thought of
her as my   sometimes mischievous   ally.

She had a special talent for imitating

voices, & often made me laugh when she
improvised conversations.

Between Hector & Andromache:

ANDROMACHE: Do you find Helen attractive,
Hector?

HECTOR: Of course.

ANDROMACHE: But you're not attracted to
her?

HECTOR: Of course not.

ANDROMACHE: Poor Helen, the only man
worth having is the only man she can't
have...

Another time:

ANDROMACHE: Cassandra says there'll be a
war over Helen. Do you think Helen is
worth a war?

HECTOR: Rubbish. She's not the only
adulterous queen in the world. Wars are
fought over more important issues. Such
as trade routes. As long as Troy keeps
control of the Black Sea trade there will
be no war, I promise you.

ANDROMACHE: I want you to promise me
something else, Hector. I want you to
promise me that you'll stay home if it
should come to a war over Helen. You're
going to be a father soon...

HECTOR: Thank you, my love...

Between her & me:

MY VOICE: My predictions have no credit in
the very presence of the catastrophe.

HELEN'S NATURAL VOICE: I'm sorry if I look
　　like a catastrophe, Cassandra.
MY VOICE: It's not your fault. You're only a
　　puppet. If you love us you'll leave us...

　　Between my parents:
HECABE: I'm worried, Priam. Cassandra has
　　been rolling her eyes again.
PRIAM: Do you want me to lock her up? &
　　place a guard outside her room, to tell us
　　what she says?
HECABE: No, don't lock her up. It wouldn't
　　look right... our own daughter... I wish
　　she'd get married. Young Othryoneus is
　　madly in love with her...
PRIAM: A penniless aristocrat with no land to
　　his name. No daughter of mine...
HECABE: Corebus is in love with her too.
　　You've seen Corebus, the prince who
　　arrived from Phrygia last week...
PRIAM: Yes, I've seen Corebus. But he's not
　　man enough for her. I want Cassandra
　　to marry her cousin Eurypylus of Mysia.
HECABE: I don't think Cassandra likes
　　Eurypylus, Priam.
PRIAM: She doesn't have to like him. All she
　　has to do is marry him. Mysia has a
　　powerful army... Just in case she's right
　　about a war....

　　Actually I was very fond of my cousin
Eurypylus. He was one of the few members of
my family who didn't try to reform me. We

became engaged at my father's insistence after he placed his Mysian army at our disposal. But I kept postponing the wedding date. Not out of spite, as Priam scolded. Nor because I was afraid of becoming pregnant & bearing a child, as Hecabe said to my sister Polyxena. Who told me. I didn't want to contaminate Eurypylus' fate with mine, by becoming his wife. I didn't want him to be killed by the Greeks because of me.

He was killed anyway. By Achilles' son Neoptolemus. Who also killed my faithful Corebus, on the last day of the war, when Corebus tried to rescue me from the rapist Ajax.

Corebus had continued to love me & still wanted to marry me after I became Agamemnon's 'concubine'. After he had seen me walk around Troy pregnant with the twins.

I still shudder at the memory of his eyes boring into mine, as he embraced one of the columns in Athena's temple, slowly sliding to his knees.

& I've never stopped shuddering at the memory of my brother Helenus my once-beloved twin who befriended Achilles' murderous son, & sailed away with him after Troy's defeat.

To Molossia. Whose king Phoenix my brother replaced, after Neoptolemus killed him for his friend, to vacate the throne.

Helenus remained King of Molossia for the fifty years he continued to live. —He lived to be eighty-three.— He founded a new capital, & married Neoptolemus' mother, Achilles' widow Deidameia.

—If Deidameia *was* Neoptolemus' mother. I cannot bear to think that the monster might have been Iphigeneia's son. Especially if Iphigeneia was the secret oldest daughter of my friend Helen.

Neoptolemus went wild, on that hideous last day. He impaled our brother Polites on his dripping sword. & he beheaded our old father Priam who threw himself across his path to save Polites.

Polites had always been my father's pride because he could run like the wind. Faster than Achilles.

Neoptolemus dragged our father's headless body to his own father's tomb. Where he left it to rot. To be joined later by the sacrificed naked body of our sister Polyxena.

& he hurled our little nephew to his death. Astynax, Hector's little son. Splitting the child's skull on the rocks that lay below our fallen city, in front of the child's mother. Andromache, who had been made a widow by his father Achilles, & whom the son was packing off as his share of the loot.

I had not been dead for very long when I recognized Andromache's voice echoing through the underworld, calling on Hector's ghost every time his murderer's son bedded down with her. But Hector's ghost was still whirling around the fallen walls of our ruined city, repeating the insult that had been done to his dead body. Which Achilles had attached to a pair of horses   by leather thongs threaded through the tendons of my dead brother's heels. My dead brother Hector had been dragged around the city for three days & three nights. His ghost's black hair was powdered grey with dust. He didn't hear his widow's cries for help.

Andromache had not been one of my favorite people. But the echo of her despair cut through the continuous rehearsal of my own unfair fate. At least I had been raped only once   —not counting Apollo's spitting into my mouth. & the man whose twins I had borne had not killed anyone I loved.

In fact, if it had been up to Agamemnon, there would have been no war.

He had persuaded his brother Menelaus to send envoys to Troy to ask for Helen's return before he agreed to raise an army. When my father sent the envoys back empty-handed, asking instead for the return of my aunt Hesione, Agamemnon continued to negotiate. Through nine years of the siege. It was my father's stubborn refusal to give up Helen   who repeated that she would prefer to leave rather than be the cause of continued bloodshed   that kept the Greeks before Troy. & finally caused the city to fall.

Helen quietly tried to scale the south wall, one night, shortly after Paris' death. She would have gone to Menelaus' tent, to humble herself before him, to plead with him to take her back & lift the siege, if my father had not discovered her absence.

Perhaps there had not yet been enough corpses to satisfy the gods. Or perhaps we had been adding to the population at too fast a rate. I was certainly guilty of adding two little boys. & Helen was even guiltier. She had born Paris a daughter & three sons. Although all three of them had just died the week before, in an accident, when the roof of a house fell on them in the servants' quarters, where they had been crawling in the courtyard while their nurse milked a goat for them.

At any rate, the gods made sure that Helen did not stop the war that night. Which was the night my father chose to go to her apartments, to convince her to marry Deiphobus, now that Paris was dead.

When he didn't find her in her rooms he limped about the palace, calling:
Helen...Helen...in a voice cracked with anguish that sent us all running, looking for her.

One of the sentinels finally spotted her: hanging in mid air half down the outside of the south wall, by a rope she had tied around her waist, groping with her toes for a foothold from which to jump onto a rock, & to the ground.

Deiphobus pulled her back up, inside our city. My father wept when he saw her, slowly walking back to the palace, with Deiphobus' arm around her shoulders.

I'm sure now that my father believed to the very end that Troy would never fall. But there were moments   at Hector's funeral, & later, after Paris' death & Helen's aborted escape; after Achilles killed my youngest brother Troilus, aged nineteen & a half, & my father still seemed to feel that we were winning   when I had the sickening suspicion that he was perhaps no longer in possession of his reason. That he wanted Troy to be destroyed, to have his world come to an end because his life was coming to an end.
I saw him like Cronus, devouring his children.

Achilles, too, was ready to negotiate a truce after he met my sister Polyxena, during the first winter of the siege.
The very evening of their encounter he sent a messenger to Hector, asking: on what terms he might marry her.
Betray the Greek camp to my father, & she is yours: was Hector's laconic reply.

This may sound as though my sister had not been consulted. That she was being treated like an object of barter, & would have been obliged to submit to whatever terms might be agreed upon, whether she liked Achilles, or not.

The truth is: Polyxena would have gone
to live with Achilles on no terms at all. On
Achilles' terms, which would have meant
sharing his heroic hulk with a number of
others, not all of them women.

I was present when she & Achilles first
caught sight of each other. In Thymbra, in
Apollo's temple. My cousin Eurypylus was also
there. He had accompanied my mother,
Polyxena, & me, to make sure we   I   would
not be molested by any roving sacrificing
Greeks. He was engaged to me then, & often
worried that Apollo might come back for more
than just another spitting kiss.

It has been said that I was jealous of my
sister Polyxena. Who was my mother's favorite
daughter, & her confidante.

Polyxena's beauty was of the readily
identifiable ultra-feminine type   prominent
bosom / narrow waist / rolling hips   which had
become the ideal of my time & area. In reaction
to the broad-shouldered narrow-hipped   often
flat-chested   Amazon beauty that went
completely out of fashion with the death of
Queen Penthesileia.

Penthesileia had briefly fought on our
side, at the beginning of the war. She had
chased Achilles around our walls a number of
times, until she tripped, & he killed her. &

stripped her dead body of its armor, as was the custom. Before he raped it   as was not the custom   in full view of Greek & Trojan soldiers.

His own people took their disgust with his conduct out on the defenseless body. Which they mutilated horribly, & threw into the Scamander river when they were finally through with it. My father had it fished out during the night, & buried inside our walls.

The skeleton of the Amazon Queen Penthesileia still lies buried amidst the ruins of my city, her courage rarely sung, while Achilles' glory grows with each retelling of his legend, & his mother Thetis continues to scratch Zeus' chin under his beard, on paintings that show her stripped to the waist. ... A narrow waist, a prominent bosom...

I fitted neither the Amazon nor the ultra-feminine type. I was neither flat-chested nor opulent. I was no type at all. Even as a mother   of twins   I continued to look like an adolescent boy.

Which delighted Agamemnon. Mine was the beauty of pure art, he used to tell me, which nature envied & seldom managed to imitate.

I often thought that he liked me so much   & continued to like me for so long because my body permitted him to satisfy a taste for boys in which he had never indulged. Which he had kept concealed from himself because it conflicted with his image of himself as a father. Not only of children, but of the people of Mycenae.

He certainly was a devoted father to the twins. Gentler, much more loving than I was a mother.

I loved Pelops & Teledamus in my fashion. Which didn't look like mother love to most people. I respected them too much from the moment of their birth to talk baby talk to them, nor did I gush over their first word or step.

I had a feeling of guilt mixed with compassion for these two new lives that had grown out of my moment of abandon. To which I had perhaps had no right. Perhaps motherhood was unnatural for me. My crime against nature. I felt estranged from myself while I was pregnant, & would gladly have gone into hiding until it was all over. I used to run from my mother Hecabe's sudden solicitude, not because I felt ashamed of carrying the child   the children   of a man who was married, but not to me, as Hecabe thought   —which prompted her to assure me, over & over, that 'Agamemnon was a great king whose love was nothing to be ashamed of'—   but because I didn't like to show myself in what looked to me like a fraudulent disguise. I couldn't wait for my 'invader(s)' to come forth.

Knowledge of the future can be a hindrance for living in the present. It makes events seem anticlimactic. My mother was right, of course: I was not a 'normal woman'.

Nor did I want to be one when I looked at most of the normal women around me.

I wouldn't have wanted to trade the fate I knew awaited me for theirs, which they ignored. I had seen what lay ahead for most of them for my mother Hecabe, for Andromache, for Polyxena & have occasionally wondered how 'normally' they would have faced their day-to-day existence if most of it had been revealed to them in advance, speeded up & condensed. I'm not sure I would have wanted to trade my knowledge for their ignorance, in order to live 'normally', up to the bitter end.

The only woman with whom I might not have minded trading in retrospect might have been Helen. Although, when I think of the acquiescent sphynx legend has made of my cheerful lively friend who was perhaps wiser even than she was seductive; & a good mother besides —the ideal embodiment of the alleged female trinity— I'd just as soon be misremembered as a wild-haired but knowledgeable maniac, who told the truth. Nothing but the truth.

I became believable, after I died. After my predictions had become useless, people suddenly began remembering what they had refused to hear me say. I am quoted & misquoted whenever Troy is mentioned. —When archeologists dig up our rubble, & try on my parents' golden crowns.

I had always admired my sister Polyxena.

70

Unlike me, she never seemed to lose control of her emotions. She was, as I have said, a fashionable beauty, used to men staring at her wherever she went. But when she became aware of Achilles, staring at her from the far end of Apollo's altar, on that windy winter morning in Thymbra, her whole face collapsed. She looked almost ugly   old   almost like our old nurse used to look when she'd had too much wine: flushed to the roots of her dark hair, her mouth hanging loose, with a sagging lower lip.

It didn't occur to me then that my sister might have seen her entire relationship with Achilles, up to her own gory end, condensed into that first contact of eyes.

Which she instantly forgot, as they continued to stare their desire into each other.

Which embarrassed me.

& must also have embarrassed my cousin-fiance Eurypylus —unless he felt my embarrassment & wanted to rescue me— because his hand was on my elbow, drawing me outside the temple. Outside the magnetic field that had begun to vibrate around Polyxena & Achilles, inside which a third person stood like an intruder.

Hecabe stayed where she was. Perhaps she was too concentrated on the ritual of the sacrifice she was preparing to notice what was happening around her. Or perhaps she enjoyed feeling surrounded by desire, even when   or perhaps all the more because   it was not focused on her. It allowed her to participate

71

without being expected to react.

Hecabe didn't share my need for privacy in sexual matters, as I discovered later, when I was pregnant with the twins. When she kept asking me what Agamemnon liked to do to me, & what he liked to have done.

She felt hurt when I wouldn't tell her anything. She was my mother! She had a right the duty to know these things. In which she could have advised me.

She may have felt that it was natural for a mother to share in the passion of her favorite daughter, & of a hero to whom gossip attributed every conceivable form of sexual inclination. Which both of them may have found as exciting as I found it repulsive.

Unless Hecabe was unable to leave the temple unable to move because she had looked into Achilles' staring eyes & had been hypnotized by a flash vision of my sister's pointless murder across his grave.

—Which was a dress rehearsal of a new custom that was being established in our area of the world. Which demanded that the widow follow her husband into death. Preferably voluntarily: by throwing herself onto his funeral pyre, or letting herself be buried alive in the same grave, next to the dead husband's body.

—Because a used hymen was not worthy of re-use by another patriarch. No grass will grow again where a widow's foot has stepped...

72

I myself saw Polyxena's end only years later. When I continued to see it   from different angles   as my visions of Troy's last days accelerated, & often overlapped, focusing on different aspects of the same event.

Until I was forced to watch it happen. Standing next to Agamemnon, who was trying his utmost to prevent it.

His unpopular conservative protest: that dead heroes had no right to live women...

Hadn't there been enough bloodshed? ... was drowned in catcalls.

Which changed to cheers when Achilles' son Neoptolemus pointed his spear at me with a twisted grin, & accused Agamemnon of preferring my 'couch' to the last wish of his heroic father.

Whose ghost   he said   had appeared to him in a dream, complaining that he was being deprived of his rightful share of the spoils.

Agamemnon looked ill as he watched Neoptolemus undress my wide-eyed sister with his spear, & jam it through her left breast, into her heart. He was afraid that I, too, would be speared if he said another word.

He hurried me off to the tent when I expressed the hope that Achilles' heroic ghost enjoyed the sight of my sister's naked body.

—Which had fallen backwards, across my father's headless body that had been lying on the grave for over a day, & had begun to smell. My father's open neck was black with flies. The sky was black with clouds of birds.

Agamemnon put his arms around me, in
the half-dismantled tent, & called me his
'reckless doe'.
I was absurdly brave to have stayed by
his side   —because I loved Him? —   he said. &
absurdly modest when I assured him that it had
taken very little courage, since I knew that
nothing was going to happen to me at Achilles'
grave. That I was going to die in another place,
at another time.

Which was not far off.
He might find me less courageous when
we arrived in Mycenae. —Where all four of us
were going to die within the hour of our arrival:
I told him once again.
Again he didn't hear me. His shield had
crashed to the ground. He stooped to pick it up,
his neck & face turning crimson with the effort.
I started packing   absurdly   for a voyage into
death.

—Something insignificant always seemed
to prevent Agamemnon from hearing me when
I tried to warn him about Mycenae.
The first time   when he did hear me;
when I was still pregnant with the twins   he
interpreted my vision of our murderous
reception as a concubine's natural reluctance to
meet the lawful wife. He kissed me on the
nose, swearing that I had no reason to be

jealous of Clytemnestra. He had not known
what love was before he met me.
    Clytemnestra's lover Aegisthus was
probably just as reluctant to meet the lawful
husband, he smiled, who was moreover still the
king. He would forgive Clytemnestra her lover,
& she would be glad to receive me. I had
nothing to fear...

    Legend has generously expanded the
virtues of Achilles, complementing his factual
physical prowess not only with   also factual
    courage, but with integrity & nobility.
However, during his lifetime   & mine   his
unusual strength was thought to be
complemented mainly by his unusual sexual
appetites.
    Which may   as I have said   have
increased his attraction in the eyes of 'normal'
women. To whom a blond muscled giant looked
heroic, & therefore desirable by definition.
Whereas I could never have let myself be loved
by anyone who looked at other women   &
men   while wanting me 'also'.
    But then, I found most heroes
unbearably pompous. They never tired of
divulging the secret of their success. Which I'd
feel prompted to counter by reminding them
that: a *hero* used to be a dead king who had been
sacrificed to *Hera* ...   I didn't feel 'honored' when
their fleeting fancy focused on my person.
    —I seemed to mistake failure for a sign of
modesty: my mother Hecabe often said. With a

75

sigh. Underdogs were notoriously vicious
biters: she'd say: & they aired their arrogance at
home . . .

One hero whom I did admire was
Palamedes. Even though he fought against
us   —until Odysseus falsely accused him of
being a secret agent in my father's pay, &
persuaded Agamemnon to have him stoned to
death.
        Palamedes had invented many useful
things: the alphabet   measures   scales   light-
houses. Even dice & card games which
kept the Greek soldiers from rioting out
of boredom & homesickness   during the
long years of the siege.
        —Which became heroic mainly in
retrospect, since sedentary poets like to glorify
dead men of action.
        Palamedes' intelligence humiliated
Odysseus' cunning. It made Odysseus feel like
the trickster he was.

I contrived to meet Palamedes when he
came to Troy as one of Agamemnon's three
envoys, to negotiate Helen's return to Sparta.
When Agamemnon was still hoping to prevent
the war by recovering its pretext, & calling
everybody's bluff.
        Which made him & his three envoys
extremely unpopular, with Greeks & Trojans
alike.
        Perhaps Agamemnon was as stubbornly

arrogant as I was   & in a far better position to
be stubborn & arrogant, as the rich king of
Mycenae   when he tried to contradict public
opinion. Which may be the gods' means of
expressing their intentions. We tend to
underestimate the power of banality.

The three envoys were staying at my
uncle Antenor's house. Where I went in secret
to meet Palamedes, disguised as a boy of the
people, carrying a cluster of fish slung over one
shoulder.
All of Troy was in the streets.
Screaming: that they weren't going to give
Helen back. Helen had come to Troy of her
own free will. The Greeks hadn't given back
my aunt Hesione, who had been forcibly
abducted, & made a slave. The envoys should
be killed, & their heads sent back to
Agamemnon, to show him that Troy was ready
to fight. For Helen   for honor   for justice...
My uncle had posted sentinels around his
house, at Palamedes' suggestion. I had to make
one of them call out the cook who knew me &
recognized me, & pretended to want to buy my
fish, before I was let in.
I couldn't tell how old Palamedes was.
He looked about the same age as my brother
Hector. But apparently he was much older,
because my father had called him 'a traitor to
his generation' for saying to him that 'fathers
were sometimes overgenerous with the lives of
their sons'...

77

I had always seen my father return from
negotiations in a satisfied, if not triumphant
frame of mind, having either obtained what he
had set out to claim, or else retained what was
being claimed from him.

He had categorically refused to give up
Helen. Yet, he came back from his meeting
with the Greek envoys looking like a beaten old
man. All that was to follow seemed to be
written in his face.

I knew that Palamedes was a prophet
  besides being a genius   & wondered what
else he might have said to my father. If
he foresaw what I foresaw. I felt that I had to
speak with him. Perhaps he would help me save
Troy.

I found him in my uncle's private
chamber, leaning against a column, watching
the street. My uncle led me up to him,
stressing my eagerness to meet a great inventor
to apologize for my get-up.

He shook his head. He felt unworthy of
the risk I had taken to make his acquaintance,
he said. All the more since he had miserably
failed in his mission. If he were as clever as his
inventions had misled me to believe he would
have known how to persuade my father to give
up Helen, instead of antagonizing him.

I said: But Helen was willing to go back
to Menelaus. She had told me so herself. More
than once.

Helen & I had become close friends, I

said. There was still hope if we could find a
way to sneak her out of the palace, & out of the
city.

Disguised as a boy? he smiled, shaking
his head.

Helen might be willing to become a
fishwife for a couple of hours . . . for a night, I
said. She might enjoy imitating the voice of a
fishwife.

Did he know that Helen had a special
talent for imitating voices?

He shook his head again, motioning with
his chin toward the noisy street.

Mob is not the plural of man, he said.
We're dealing with a different species, that has
kaleidoscopes in the hollows of the eyes. Where
projections of violence keep rotating at
increasing velocity. Until the prisms shatter
with their own frenzy, & the blinded creature
collapses in the rubble it has created.

It was all an extension of the weather,
Palamedes said. Which the individual might be
able to resist. & at times even use to his
advantage. But collectively, men merely
reacted.

Mob behavior was nothing but an
amplification of storms, & landslides, & shifts in
temperature. Collectively, men were like
roaches, only less resilient. Less intelligent, if
survival was a criterion of intelligence.

Below a certain temperature roaches
retreated into dark corners, & sallied forth
individually, to forage for bread & dairy

products. Individually, roaches were vegetarians. But when the weather turned hot, they came out in swarms, & turned carniverous. Even cannibalistic, if it got hot enough & there was not enough other meat around. Preferring to eat each other even if there was...

Listen to them out there. You don't argue with the voice of the mob: he said. Prophetically advising himself.

Foreknowledge didn't save him from Odysseus' stones. Not any more than it saved me from Clytemnestra's ax.

Few seers seem to know how to act on their insights. Calchas was one of the few who knew. & my traitor-twin Helenus, although it was resentment more than knowledge that ultimately 'saved' Helenus. Or rather, his resentment prompted him to act on the knowledge he had had all along.

Truth, I mourn you who have predeceased me: were Palamedes' last words, before the stones overwhelmed him.

Agamemnon repeated them to me. Asking himself if he had witnessed & sanctioned the death of a hero, not the execution of a traitor. Was it better to let a criminal go free than to punish an innocent man?

Strangely enough, Agamemnon might have saved himself from being murdered & perhaps even me, & the twins if he had saved

Palamedes.

    Causality makes strange connections.
Without the help of her lover Aegisthus
Clytemnestra might not have had the courage
to kill her husband. & she might not have
taken a lover without the persuasive advice of
Palamedes' father Nauplius, who traveled from
palace to palace, all through Greece, inciting the
lonely wives of the warriors before Troy to
commit adultery, to avenge the death of his
son...

    It is not surprising that legend honors
Palamedes far less than his murderer Odysseus.
    Or than Achilles, my sister's golden-
haired idol.
    Whose sexual peculiarities she
painstakingly tried to explain to me. By his
peculiar childhood.
    In the care of a centaur Cheiron who
raised the infant on hero food. On the innards
of lions & bears & stags. & taught it hero skills:
endurance...swiftness...music...the art of
healing. At the age of four Achilles could run
faster than a stag.
    Which he began to run down & strangle,
at the age of five.
    The golden-curled boy had the instincts
of a killer of a hunter, my sister preferred to
call it which his four-legged tutor vainly tried
to curb. By changing the hero-diet to fruit &
honey. & making the sulking boy bury the
strangled beasts whose carcasses he kept

81

dragging back to the cave in which they lived, in stubborn expectation of praise.

Achilles had been Thetis' seventh son. But he was the only one to survive his mother's efforts to immortalize her children with a mortal husband by burning away their mortal parts, or by immersing them in the river Styx.

Later, Polyxena tried to explain Achilles' aversion to bathing by his mother's attempt to drown him in the Styx.

Apparently he rarely used water, & preferred to oil & perfume his body. He would arrive at their secret meetings smelling like a room full of hetaerae, she'd tell me with an excited giggle.

I'm afraid I showed little understanding for my sister's excitement. To me, Achilles was the portrait of his name. Which means: Lipless. & that was exactly how he looked to me: a giant blond baby with a hyphen for a mouth.

Which I interpreted as an indication of humorless selfishness.

Polyxena became quite annoyed when I said so. She insisted that Achilles had been named 'Lipless' because, as a baby, he'd never had the chance to use his little lips on his immortal mother's or any mortal nurse's breasts.

He was making up for that though, she added, blushing & giggling.

A name was the capsule which contained a person's character, I insisted. She'd better watch out.

She asked me in an annoyed tone of voice if that was why our mother preferred to call me: Alexandra. A woman who fought off men...

Obviously I wasn't in love with Agamemnon, or I'd understand how one's whole body became alert with desire.

All her senses had become keener, since she'd met Achilles. Her eyes, her sense of smell. Everything she did with him, or for him, every ordinary little gesture acquired a new, almost ceremonial significance. Which left her feeling breathless. & opulent.

Everything Achilles did excited her, she said. Especially certain things which some people found peculiar. That he wore jewelry, for instance. The contrast of earrings & ankle bracelets & long thin golden chains on his tall strong heavily perfumed body made her shiver with anticipation. Just thinking of it made her shiver. It made her feel that he came to their meetings adorned as for a sacred ritual.

...In which he expected to sacrifice or to be sacrificed? I asked.

She didn't laugh. Obviously I'd never been in love...

My sister's infatuation with Achilles did not seem to conflict with her love of Troy. But I don't think that she used Achilles' infatuation with her to betray him, as his son Neoptolemus & his increasingly heroic legends have claimed.

—At least not until Achilles killed our

youngest brother Troilus who had always been her favorite brother.

I think Polyxena was merely acting out the role Achilles had assigned to her in the passion play they kept playing with & for each other, against the backdrop of the war, when she dramatically stripped off her heavy golden bracelets, & tossed them into the lighter scale, under the   unusually short   nose of Achilles, who was selling our brother Hector's abused dead body to my father for its weight in gold.

An enormous scale had been set up outside the south gate. Achilles was standing in front of it. I saw him turn ashen when my sister threw the bracelets into the top scale. Which Achilles started pulling down with both hands, making it level with the other scale in which Hector's heavy body had been placed.

He was satisfied: he said.

Then he begged my father to let him marry Polyxena. Promising to end the war on the day of their wedding.... if my father agreed to give back Helen ...

My father agreed to give him Polyxena —but not to give back Helen—   on the day he ended the war ...

The war continued. Polyxena continued to meet Achilles in secret. & to tell me about him. & to offer explanations for his peculiarities.

His peculiar adolescence, spent as a girl among girls ...

Achilles' mother Thetis had been watching over her only surviving son from a distance.

When he turned eleven   & had killed some three-thousand   bears   boars   lions stags   she consulted an oracle about his future. She was told that Achilles would not return from Troy where he would, however, earn immortalizing glory. But he could also live a long, but unglorious life if he was kept away from Troy.

It may seem illogical that a mother who had burned or drowned six sons for the sake of immortality, & had almost burned or drowned the seventh, would choose to save that seventh son from a glorifying though early death.

But that was what Thetis tried to do. She dressed the tall muscled twelve-year-old in girl's clothes, & took him to her friend Lycomedes, the king of Scyros.   Among whose twelve daughters Achilles spent the next three years of his life as a thirteenth girl, under the name of Pyrrha.

Which did not prevent him from having an amorous intrigue with one of the twelve daughters.   Deidameia, who became the mother of his monster-son Neoptolemus.

—As I have said: I prefer to believe that Deidameia was the mother of Neoptolemus, & not Iphigeneia.   Especially if Iphigeneia was Helen's daughter.

Troy might still be standing   a modernized ancient city like Athens or Rome, more ancient than Athens or Rome   if Achilles had continued to live & love as Pyrrha in Lycomedes' palace in Scyros.

If Odysseus had not tricked him out of his girl's disguise with a gift   —which seems to have been Odysseus' recipe; this time a gift of arms—   for which the unusual girl reached with undisguised delight. Whereupon Odysseus triumphantly brought the fifteen-year-old Achilles to Agamemnon. Who felt obliged to give him the command of the Greek fleet.

Agamemnon & Achilles were not particularly fond of each other. They communicated as little as possible; mainly through Odysseus.

Agamemnon often told me about the petulance of Achilles. Who bore him a grudge because he rightly suspected that he had been made commander of the fleet solely at the insistence of Calchas, the Trojan traitor-seer who knew that Troy could not be taken without the 'assistance' of Achilles.

I've mentioned Calchas a number of times. For over three thousand years he rarely was absent from my memory. But I've put off speaking about him in greater detail because I still haven't been able to decide whether he was an opportunist, or a wise detached prophet who was following divine orders.

I realize that the gift of prophecy is not necessarily coupled with a high sense of morality. Many seers are greedy, cowards who shamelessly slant their interpretations to gain personal advantage. Who set themselves up as saviors of humanity, after they've run from debts & family obligations, & changed their names.

But I had known Calchas all my life. I had gone to his house & played with his daughter Briseis after her mother died. When Briseis was still a little girl. & after Troilus fell in love with her   & she with him   she often came to the palace & talked with me for long hours in my room.

Calchas' repeated betrayal of my city which had been his city as much; longer
& of my father who trusted him more than he trusted me or Helenus or Aesacus   still stuns me as much as when I first heard that he had taken up residence in Achilles' tent outside our walls.

—Leaving his motherless daughter behind in the city he knew to be doomed.

Of course he may also have known that my father would generously let Briseis go when he asked for her two years later. Calchas did seem to be all-knowing.

To me, my father's gestures of generosity remained unpredictable. They seemed to be reserved for our enemies. Perhaps I had no conception of what losing face meant to my father, since it meant nothing to me.

I never understood why he had not killed

Achilles, on the night of their appointed barter for Hector's body, when he walked in on Achilles asleep in his tent. Achilles had just killed the most glorious of his sons. My father had every reason to avenge that son. Instead, he softly called out the sleeping killer's name, & then agreed to buy back Hector's abused dishonored —but divinely preserved— body for its weight in gold.

—Whereby my father may have been getting generously even with Apollo. If Hector *was* Apollo's son . . .

As was Troilus. Whose heart my father broke when he generously allowed Briseis to leave our city. Exquisitely torturing Troilus by ordering him to escort the girl he loved to the enemy camp. Where he would no longer be able to see her.

Briseis came to my room one last time, after her father had betrayed my father, to tell me that her father had been 'ordered' by the Delphic oracle to go over to the Greeks, & to swear an oath of friendship to Achilles.

Her father was not a traitor: she insisted: he was merely obeying the command of the gods.

—I later wondered whose command Briseis was obeying when she shifted the undying love she had sworn to my brother onto Diomedes, Odysseus' friend & assistant-in-deception, less than a month after she had gone to join her father in Achilles' tent.

      Helenus & I had warned my father many times that Troy would fall if Helen stayed. He had always shrugged us aside. But I think that his conversation with Palamedes, during the fruitless negotiation to prevent the war, while the mob chanted: Kill them   kill them   kill them   around my uncle Antenor's house, had sown a doubt in my father's mind, which he hoped the oracle would dispell when he sent Calchas to Delphi.
      Like a gout-plagued drinker who hopes that the doctor will prescribe a diet of wine, my father hoped that his refusal to surrender Helen to Agamemnon's envoys would meet with divine approval.

      —Which it did, considering that a war was what the gods intended. To rebalance life on earth by wiping Troy off the map.
      It is conceivable that the gods didn't want to take any chances with the human faculty of reason which might have sabotaged their war effort. If my father had changed his mind, for instance, & preferred to lose face rather than Troy.
      —One god in particular may have been counting on the war   if not on the defeat of Troy which he feigned to be defending   to advance his divine career. Delphi had become Apollo's oracular shrine after he slew the

original female python...

Briseis may have been telling me the truth when she said that the oracle had 'ordered' her father to run over to the Greeks. It may even have ordered him to reveal the secrets of Troy's vulnerability to them, one by one, thriftily spaced out over the years of the siege.

Calchas was a prudent man. He gave out his revelations sparingly, & kept the Greeks in need of him until the very end.

The siege could not succeed without the presence of Achilles.

The city could not be invaded as long as the Palladium remained within our walls.

My family could not be deposed if Troilus reached the age of twenty.

The god-made walls of Troy could not be taken by force, only by ruse...

I refused to believe Briseis, & it was the end of our friendship. I told her that I thought her father had used his authorized absence from our doomed city not to come back. He'd had no need to go to Delphi to be told that Troy would fall if Helen stayed. He & Helenus & I, & our halfbrother Aesacus   had known that all along.

Her prompt betrayal of my brother Troilus reinforced my low opinion of Calchas. Like father, like daughter: I thought. An unimaginative attitude which I would have refuted with passion if anyone had applied it to me.

—It never was applied to me. My 'sin' was: being different...

The humiliating, almost ridiculous cause of Calchas' death   injured vanity   further seemed to confirm his lack of stature. If the way in which we die is any indication   the culmination   of the way in which we have lived.

—I used to think that it was. & sometimes went as far as taking pride in the foreknowledge of Clytemnestra's ax dramatically severing my head. In my own ridiculous vanity.

Calchas' death had been predicted. I had known for some time that he would outlive Troy only by months. By a year at most. That he would travel by land to Colophon, where he would meet his end. But I didn't know that the great seer Mopsus, the son of Tiresias' daughter Manto, would be the cause.

When Calchas met the great Mopsus in Colophon he felt compelled to challenge him to an accuracy contest. He asked Mopsus to predict the number of figs that were going to be harvested from a certain tree that was standing nearby, heavy with fruit.

Mopsus' reply was accurate down to a single fig.

Challenged in turn to predict the number of piglets inside the belly of a pregnant sow Calchas guessed: Eight young boars.

When the sow gave birth to two young sows & one boar, the next day at noon, Calchas fell dead of a broken heart.

Into the sow's trough in the pigsty.

The whole underworld greeted his arrival with laughter. Except for me. I had just recently arrived myself & didn't feel in a laughing mood. I had laughed too hard   too much off key   during the crossing to Mycenae.

I don't know what became of Calchas. I was never able to find him when I went in search of him, to hear from himself what made him betray us. Perhaps he has been avoiding me for over three thousand years.

Unless   unlike me   he became reabsorbed into a new form of life almost immediately.

—I have been told that the very evolved & the first-timers usually are reborn at once. In keeping with the principle of life, which is continuity in change.

Which functions on two levels:

Amoral matter. That loves the rat as much as the hero. As much as the ground both of them fertilize after they destroy each other.

& absolutely moral spirit. That lets each living form express its essence until pure formlessness is reached.

But punishes the rebel mind that understood its light   or fire   & stole it, to give away to unenlightened fellow men, by

embalming the rebel identity until it is ground
smooth again by the friction of time.

     I don't mean to suggest that my father
was intentionally cruel to Troilus when he
ordered him to take Briseis to her father in
Achilles' tent. Instead of sending one of my
other brothers. Or halfbrothers. He knew
that Troilus & Briseis were in love. He may
have thought that he was doing them a favor,
allowing them to be together as long as
possible.
     He could, of course, have refused to let
Briseis go. She was weeping, begging him to
allow her to stay with Troilus. But, as I have
said, my father was extremely generous toward
his enemies. Condescendingly generous,
perhaps. By betraying him, Calchas had placed
himself in the receiving position.
     & of course my father could not know
that the Greek Diomedes would replace Troilus
in Briseis' affection in less than a month. &
that Diomedes would try to kill the rival he had
supplanted whenever Troilus showed himself
on the battlefield.
     Where Troilus was showing himself
much too openly, much too often, after Briseis'
departure. Courting not only his death   at age
nineteen   but the defeat of Troy which, as I
had foretold, could not be taken if Troilus
reached the age of twenty.
     Nor could my father   or anybody   have

imagined that Achilles would catch sight of Troilus, sorrowfully delivering Briseis to his tent, & that he would fall madly in love with him.

For which my sister Polyxena failed to find an explanation in his peculiar upbringing that had heretofore supplied her with plausible reasons for almost anything Achilles used to do.

For his passionate attachment to Patroclus, for instance, his older, less-wellborn cousin from Locria, which had kept the servants snickering since the beginning of the siege.

My sister had mourned with Achilles when Hector killed Patroclus.

& so had I, because I knew that grief & the desire for revenge would send Achilles back to the battlefield from which he had withdrawn after the windy winter morning when he first met Polyxena in Thymbra. I knew that Achilles would not rest until he had killed our brother Hector.

Patroclus' death did put an abrupt end to the truce. During which the Greek soldiers had played with Palamedes' cards & dice, or watched shoulder to shoulder with Trojan soldiers while Paris & Menelaus fought duels over the possession of their wife Helen, & the treasures she had brought to Troy.

A spectacle which the gods also enjoyed watching. In which they could not resist interfering. At one point, Aphrodite shrouded my brother Paris in her misty veil & whisked him back to his bedroom in the palace when it seemed that Menelaus was about to gain the upper hand. Legend has called Paris a coward ever since.

According to Homer, Achilles & Patroclus were bound by the noblest of friendships, based on mutual devotion & protection. As though their first physical contact had occurred only after the flesh, when Achilles' ashes were mixed with the ashes of his beloved cousin, as had been his wish.

Before it occurred to his insatiable ghost̩ or to his insatiably murderous son to claim union in death also with my as-yet-alive sister Polyxena.

I'm not unfamiliar with Homer's censorships. He omitted the most important aspect of *my* life my clairvoyance & describes me merely as 'a beautiful golden-haired Trojan princess'. Out of kindness to my memory, I think. Knowledge was no longer a flattering attribute for a woman, at the time of his writing.

Whereas homosexuality at least among men had become far less of a scandal than during Achilles' & my lifetime. Contemporaries of Homer were sculpting statues of the legendary giant, wearing a woman's earring in his left ear, as an additional attraction to his modern, more evolved admirers. Who had less & less admiration for the women they slept with, except as the mothers of their sons.

Perhaps Homer was shocked by the

simultaneity of Achilles' various passions. &
afraid to corrupt future generations by passing
on the truth.

I admit: I was shocked at first when
Polyxena showed me the lust letters he wrote
to her, begging her to meet him, long after he
had begun chasing our brother Troilus around
the battlefield, in front of sheepishly grinning
soldiers. Without the slightest concern even for
ridicule, since his visible passion for Troilus was
visibly unrequited.

At least he was protecting Troilus from
Diomedes, I said to Polyxena who was
beginning to complain about Achilles' lack of
propriety. Perhaps he felt that a hero such as
he had no need to bother with conventions, I
said. At least he wasn't a hypocrite.

What did *I* know! *I* had never been in
love! & I didn't know how lucky I was to have
Agamemnon. She was crying: She wasn't going
to meet Achilles any more . . .

I don't know if Troilus could have saved
himself   & Troy   if he had given in to Achilles.

I'm not suggesting that he should have
given in. Or that he could have. As I have said:
I found Achilles repulsive. But the impact of
Achilles' embrace might not have been fatal, if
my brother had let himself be approached.
Instead of trying to run from a giant who had
outrun & overtaken stags. If he had not
continued running from the giant in open
country   fleeing toward Thymbra, toward the

shrine of his father Apollo.

Who did not intervene when Achilles
overtook my brother, & crushed him to death,
in the satisfaction of his long pent-up desire.

I realize that my sister was seeking
revenge for herself as much as for Troilus
who had been her favorite brother when
she sent the messenger who brought the
news of Troilus' death directly to Achilles'
tent with a note, agreeing to meet him
'now that her rival was dead'. & that she was
acting out the last scene of their peculiar love
drama when she asked him to come 'to the place
of their first encounter' dressed as a woman,
barefoot, & wearing his ankle bracelets.

I know that will excite him: she
whispered to me. I know he'll come.

I said nothing to stop her. For the first
time since the beginning of their relationship I
understood her wish to meet Achilles.

—In Thymbra. Where the crucial
moments of our lives seem to have been
concentrated, as though we had lived to be
revived in plays. Facilitating the task of future
playwrights by supplying unity of place.

Legend accuses my sister of
'treacherously plotting' Achilles' 'murder'. &
our 'cowardly' brother Paris of 'ignominiously'
shooting a poisoned arrow into Achilles' right
heel, his only vulnerable spot   (Helenus had
shot a poisoned arrow into Achilles' hand two

years before, but it had bounced off without piercing the skin)   which my 'devious: typically female' sister 'cajoled' out of the 'trusting' hero to reveal to her abject accomplice who was hiding behind Apollo's divine   probably grinning   image.

Until quite recently the injustice of posterity used to outrage me. What need had legend to condemn Paris & Polyxena   & even its otherwise adored Helen: of adultery & theft of Sparta's treasures (which were her property!) —   while applauding Odysseus & Diomedes for stealing our Palladium, the protective 'luck of Troy'. In their case, legend speaks admiringly of the thieves'   of Odysseus' 'ingenuity'.

Was legend trying to justify fate retroactively   —even after the gods that had decreed the fate had fallen—   by turning the winners into high-minded heroes, & the Trojan losers into weaklings whose questionable morals had invited the defeat.

—With an honorable mention thrown in for my brother Hector & his virtuous Andromache.—

As though our lives had not been unfair enough.

I seethed with indignation when Achilles & Odysseus became the alpha & omega of legendary hero worship   Achilles, the glorious body, & Odysseus, the glorious mind, the man who lived by his wits   while the equally glorious body of the Amazon Queen Penthesileia lies mangled & forgotten under the rubble of my misremembered city, & the far more glorious truly ingenious mind of Palamedes is rarely mentioned even by Greek scholars.

I can hear the echo of Palamedes' laughter rippling through the millennia. Telling me not to delay my metamorphosis for the sake of a reputation that has long ceased to matter even to himself. Advising me to watch the way history is written. & rewritten. By one country about others. By new governments about the old ones which they are replacing. Clothing & reclothing the ghosts of one-time facts to suit whatever truth & justice happen to be in fashion.

Teasing me that women & wisemen have little mob appeal, except as martyrs. & that truth & justice are without past, present, or future. There is no reason for them to come to life after their murderers have died.

It is fortunate for Odysseus that legend stresses his mind, & rarely describes his body. Stating discreetly that 'he looked nobler when seated'. Without specifying that he turned into a bow-legged dwarf when he stood up.

Odysseus looked like a convincing beggar even in his own exaggeratedly homespun— clothes. No wonder Penelope drew her veil down over her eyes as she left for Ithaca with him.

Penelope was a sophisticated Spartan woman, & her main reason for wishing to leave her native city   disobeying her father who was imploring the newly weds to stay, in keeping with matrilocal Spartan tradition   was not because Odysseus had convinced her that it had become proper for a modern wife to follow her husband, as was soon to become the new custom throughout the world, but because she wanted to remove herself from the over-shadowing presence of her cousin Helen who had just become Queen of Sparta. & insisted on calling her: Duckie . . .

Perhaps Odysseus' vindictive sense of ridicule which often prompted him to add insult to injury may be explained to some extent by his unusual proportions.

There are many conflicting stories about how Odysseus contrived to steal the Palladium. The one that glorifies not only his legendary cunning, but also his courage   his willingness to endure pain for the sake of a worthy cause: the defeat of Troy   has him scheme his way into our city as a querulous Cretan beggar who has himself brutally flogged by the Greeks, for the benefit of gullible watching Trojans. Who then take the outcast in.

Helen who, as I have said, had an active compassion for the poor, leads the bleeding old man to her apartments & offers him food & a bath.

The bath forces Odysseus to shed his

disguise. She recognizes him, readily agrees to keep his presence in our city a secret, in exchange for her own future safety, after Troy falls. As both of them know she must.

According to some accounts Helen even gives Odysseus a golden vial which contains a sweet-tasting sleeping potion, a present to her from the king of Egypt.

At this point, my mother walks in on them. She, too, recognizes Odysseus. He throws himself at her merciful feet & convinces her that he has come to 'remove the Palladium to safety', since Troy is doomed to fall.

My mother is glad of this. She still is a Locrian at heart, & therefore feels responsible for Athena's statue which has always been guarded by Locrian priestesses, in our city. She, too, agrees to keep his presence a secret; to help him even as much as she can. Odysseus then generously promises that he will protect her when Troy falls.

In the evening Odysseus slips back into his beggar's garb, & out of the palace.

At Athena's temple he is joined by Diomedes who has entered Troy less heroically, crawling in through a muddey sewer.

Odysseus feeds Helen's sleeping potion to the watching Locrian priestess. Or else, he convinces her as he convinced my mother, that Troy is doomed & that the sacred image must be removed to safety.

The two thieves lift the Palladium off its stand & carry it away. Without being stopped

at any of the gates. Or else, heroically killing
the guard   or guards   who try to stop them.

I'll never cease to admire the skill   if not
the pragmatism   of historians & mythograph-
ers who manage to blend a number of small
truths & probabilities into one large lie.
Which hungry hero worshippers swallow
whole, without the reservation of a doubt.
It is true that my mother was of Locrian
origin. As were Athena's priestesses who
guarded the Palladium. But why would my
mother have agreed to protect Odysseus'
thieving presence in our city & help him
'remove the sacred image to safety' when she
knew that Troy could not fall as long as that
image remained within our walls. I know that
my mother knew that the safety of the image &
the safety of Troy were interdependent.
It is also true that Odysseus 'protected'
my mother after the fall of our city by claiming
her as a share of his loot.   —To his later regret,
when she turned herself into a bitch.—   But
how can anyone believe that my mother whose
whole life was her family would have offered
silence for the chance to survive the beheading
of her husband, & most of her slaughtered sons
& daughters. Even her little grandson Astynax!
Again it is true that Helen knew
Odysseus well. —The mention of his name
always made her laugh.— She certainly knew
him well enough to recognize him   probably
even before she made him shed his beggar's

102

disguise.

    & she probably would not have betrayed his presence. Not because she had 'remained loyal' to the Greeks through all the years she lived with us in Troy　—which, as legend likes to insinuate, she wanted to fall, the sooner the better, so that she could go home & become a virtuous wife again—　but because denouncing Odysseus would have required taking action. & this is something I never saw Helen do. I don't mean to say that she was passive, like the object her posthumous admirers have tried to make of her. But she never meddled, least of all to expose someone.

    It is also quite true that Odysseus liked to disguise himself. Especially as a beggar, a role for which he may have felt precast because of his proportions. & he did sneak into Troy in that disguise at least once　a number of years earlier　to find out how long our supplies might last. But not on the night of the theft of the Palladium, & it was Diomedes who physically stole it, & carried it off.

    On that night, Odysseus & Diomedes both crawled into our city through the unheroic sewer that emptied into the Scamander river.

    & it probably was Odysseus who gagged the watching priestess. Who tied her to the stand on which the Palladium had stood, in the same position in which the Palladium had stood. The priestess' right arm was painfully tied to her neck, to keep it raised above her head. Adding insult to injury...

& there is an unheroic aftermath on
which legend rarely dwells: Odysseus would
have killed his best friend & accomplice
Diomedes in order to reap the single-handed
glory of their theft, after they had crawled out
of the sewer & onto the river bank, & were
prudently making their way back to the Greek
camp, Diomedes walking ahead of Odysseus,
the Palladium still strapped to his back, if
Diomedes had not seen the shadow of
Odysseus' sword reaching for his neck, in the
light of the moon.

When he swung around, Odysseus
pretended to be cutting a branch off a tree...

Admirers of Odysseus may question my
knowledge of so much detail   especially in
situations which I had obviously not witnessed

& mockingly ask if I'm using my foreknowledge backwards.

But if they have any reason for
resentment in their lives, they must know that
one can spend much time dwelling on its causes.
Which can sometimes lead to surprising
discoveries.

I spent most of three thousand years
reliving & researching every moment of my
fate. I questioned every person who would let
me, in the underworld. Including the more
approachable of our fallen gods & goddesses.
(Most of whom were evasive, & preferred to
tell anecdotes rather than answer my
questions.) I collected hundreds of conflicting
life-stories, from which I then extracted

concurring incidents. I've come as close to the truth as facts would let me.

The well-known story of the wooden horse   in which I'm sure I recognize the imprint of my traitor-twin Helenus' mind, at least as to the structural aspect of the thing   again stresses the resourcefulness of the winners & the gullibility of the losers. But this time I cannot refute legend, except in that it gives altogether too much credit to Odysseus. As though he had conquered Troy all by himself. The gullibility of practically everyone in Troy was an appalling fact.

If understandable. My people had been used to traveling about, by land as well as by sea. Before the war, our farmers cultivated fields that lay as far as three days from our gates. & our fishermen sometimes stayed out for as long as a week. The siege had restricted their movements to the city proper, enforcing idleness & boredom.

Besides an increasing shortage of food. For the last four years we had been rationed to a daily minimum   —which I insisted on sharing, renouncing my privileges as a royal princess. The rations were keeping us alive, but for how much longer. My father assured our people in monthly speeches that we had enough grain & salted meat & fish to outwait the Greeks, but every citizen knew that there was not enough to feed us through another winter. Women of the people no longer

produced enough milk to nurse their babies.
The prospect of starving inside our god-made
storm-proof walls was beginning to cause riots
in the Southgate section, where the fishermen
lived.

It was only natural that a cry of joy went
up, on the windy October morning when our
scouts found the Greek camp lying in still
smoking ashes, & their ships gone from the
horizon. My father had been right after all: we
had outwaited the enemy. Our endurance had
won the war.

Which we might have won, still, at this
late hour, at least we might have escaped
destruction   in spite of Calchas' & Helenus'
betrayals, in spite of the theft of the Palladium
& the death of Troilus   if my father had
listened to me   or to Laocoon   & had burned
the wooden horse. On the shore where he had
limped to take a look at it.

Laocoon knew as well as I that the
gigantic contraption contained armed Greeks.
& unlike me he had a chance to make himself
believed. The spear he thrust into the
creature's flank produced an echo of rattling
armor that seemed to bear him out. He was
convincing several Trojan elders.

But at that moment Apollo   our alleged
ally   sent two large serpents that rode in on
the waves & twined themselves around
Laocoon's twin sons who had been standing on
either side of their father, & strangled them to
death.

Which all but Laocoon & me took for a foretaste of Athena's wrath, if Troy did not take in the fir-wood horse that bore a dedication to the goddess on the flank into which Laocoon had thrust his spear: "In grateful anticipation of a safe voyage home, Menelaus, Odysseus, & Neoptolemus dedicate this offering to their protectress Athena".

Laocoon vainly tried to free his sons from the serpents. Which let go only after the two young men were dead. & wound themselves around the father's arms & legs, & finally around his throat, choking the warning he was still shouting to all watching Trojans.

Apollo's intervention did not surprise me. Not even the 'coincidence' of his timing.

Apollo bore Laocoon a grudge, supposedly, for having married although he was a priest, & for lying with his wife in the Thymbran temple, where the two sons had allegedly been conceived.

Punishing his priest at that moment allowed Apollo to maintain his reputation as the noble defender of a doomed civilization, while helping to precipitate its doom.

What did surprise me was the silence of my protectress Athena. Odysseus had used her name to make his deception believable. In my opinion this was blasphemy, which rarely went unpunished for long.

But, as I have said, the gods seemed to live very slowly, compared to ourselves.

107

Athena waited for the Greeks to sail home for good, after it was all over & Troy had fallen, before she punished the blasphemers with storms & shipwrecks, & made them lose their way.

—Coincidentally punishing the Locrian Ajax for raping me in her temple.

It is also possible that Athena did not wish to antagonize the ambiguous Apollo by disrupting his punishment with a punishment of her own.

I refused to think that she, too, might have wanted Troy to fall because Paris had chosen Aphrodite.

Until her siding with Apollo in the defense of Orestes, during Orestes' trial for matricide in her very own city of Athens, I used to believe that Athena agreed with me, in my opinion of Apollo. & that she was truly on the side of Troy.

Apparently, Menelaus thought so too. Agamemnon told me that Menelaus refused to sacrifice to Athena before he & Helen sailed back to Sparta, because 'Athena had favored the Trojans for too long'...

Incidentally, Agamemnon did not take part in Odysseus' scheme. He certainly was not one of the warriors I knew to be hiding inside the belly of the horse. Although he did give the orders to burn down most of the Greek camp.

—With the exception of the tent in which

he had lived with me & the twins. Which I
found partly dismantled & carefully covered
over with earth. & when I crawled inside   as
he must have known I would   I found a letter
he had written to me, telling me that he loved
me, & that he would soon be back to 'take us
home'.

As everyone knows, my father had the
ugly horse-shaped thing dragged inside our
walls   one side of which had to be broken down
to force it through the South gate   & up to
Athena's temple in the heart of the city.
     & there it stood through half the night,
with a garland of asters around its neck,
ridiculous & threatening, while my father
opened the palace to anyone who wanted to
come, & gave a banquet which exhausted our
remaining supplies.

The only person who did not join in the
city-wide revelry was my uncle Antenor.
Not   as has been said about him   because he
had been collaborating with the Greeks, & was
soberly waiting for the feast to be over to light
a torch on the roof of his house, giving the
signal for the Greek attack when all of Troy lay
defenseless in drunken sleep. In exchange for
safeconduct for himself & his family,
supposedly.
     Supposedly Odysseus hung a leopard
skin over the entrance to my uncle's house
during the sack of our city, as a sign that

the house & those inside were to be spared. &
afterwards, Menelaus supposedly offered my
uncle one of his ships. In which he, & my
aunt, & my four cousins then sailed to the
North Italian plains, & founded the city
of Padua.

They did sail to Italy, but on a makeshift
raft which my uncle & his sons put together
after the Greeks departed, after the fall of Troy.

—Which my uncle did not witness
because he & his family were spending the
night on which he supposedly lit the torch that
signalled the propitious moment for the Greek
attack in a hut he had prepared for an
emergency, in the thickest woods on Mount
Ida.

It is true that my uncle had been
opposed to the war from the beginning. For
years he had tried   as had Agamemnon   to put
an end to the bloodshed. Arguing with my
father to let Helen go, as a gesture of goodwill
to initiate peace negotiations.

My uncle knew that the end had come
when our scouts discovered Odysseus' horse on
the deserted beach. But unlike me, he didn't
shout his knowledge into every face in sight.
He & his family quietly slipped out of Troy, &
took refuge in their hut.

He offered to take me & the twins along.
But I could not bring myself to leave. As I have
said: I felt that my life was bound up with my
city & her people. I could not keep quiet.

This time, my father finally carried out

his threat: he sequestered me in my room, with two armed guards at the entrance. I lay on my bed, yelling warnings against the horse into the mounting exuberance of the banquet.

When Helen came to free me several hours later   bearing a chunk of roast lamb & a carafe of wine   my uncle Antenor had left.

I emerged from my room behind Helen's protective back, swinging an ax. I wanted to decapitate the horse, I said, so that all could see that its belly contained what I knew it contained: armed Greeks.

To appease my father who had obviously been drinking much wine, & was looking at me as though he'd have a heart attack if I uttered another word, Helen proposed that she & Deiphobus would go with me to the horse. & that she would call out the name of every Greek warrior I'd give to her. In the voices of their wives, all of whom she had met at one time or another. The husbands would certainly answer, if they were really inside. & then Deiphobus could help me behead the horse.

Everyone knew how perfectly Helen imitated voices. The banquet hall shook with laughter & applause. & those who had not drunk too much to walk came out & trailed along behind us.

Helen liked an audience. & I was glad of every extra ear that   —as I hoped—   would hear a Greek husband call back out to what he had to mistake for his wife.

Making him wonder   with some alarm, I

hoped   how his wife had come to Troy. If indeed *he* was in Troy, inside a dark wooden box that had perhaps been dragged elsewhere, to some other unknown location where his wife happened to be. Unless he was dead, & could communicate with his wife regardless of geographical distance . . .

My hopes collapsed when Helen called Menelaus' name first. In her own natural   former-wife   voice. Which let the Greeks know that she was there, standing next to their horse   obviously in Troy   & anyone who knew Helen also knew that she had a special talent for imitating voices.

It was my own fault. For giving her Menelaus' name together with the others. Twenty-three in all. I should have realized that she would start with the name that was the most familiar to her. Perhaps, if I   & she   had started with Antielus, his cry might have been heard. Saving Troy in the last hour. If Odysseus had not been warned by Helen's voice calling Menelaus, & then his own name with the voice of his Duckie-Penelope, he might not have clapped such a ready hand over Antielus' opening mouth.

Breaking all of Antielus' teeth, & choking him to death.

Agamemnon could not forgive himself for coming back too late to save me from being raped by the Locrian Ajax. Unlike many modern husbands   or lovers   he did not accuse me of infidelity. Nor did he feel that my body had suddenly become impure. On the contrary, as I have said, the outrage of another man imposing his lust upon me seemed to have increased my desirability in his eyes. He couldn't keep his hands off me, & didn't let me out of his sight for a moment.

Not even to spare me the sight of his inability to restrain the enthusiasm of the conquering 'heroes' who were making up for ten years of tedium, plundering, burning & raping an open city.

The prospect of slavery was driving our noblewomen to madness. They lay rolling in the streets, tearing their clothes & their hair, & a great number killed their children.

My oldest sister Laodice who had had a brief affair with an Athenian before the siege, when the man had come to Troy in the retinue of Agamemnon's envoys, was so afraid that he would take her to Athens as his concubine that her loud screams reached the ears of the Great Mother Herself. She opened the earth at Laodice's feet, & took her in.

I shall not list every gratuitous murder & act of cruelty which the heroes committed during those last days. For three thousand years I relived each one down to the last detail. Crying out to our unfair gods long after they themselves had fallen.

Finally I wrote a letter to Apollo:

113

Most Fair Unfair Apollo—
Perhaps it will flatter Your Godship to receive in Your retirement the appeal of a humble mortal who has long ceased to be, yet cannot rest in peace.

Injustice has an independent life & does not always die together with its victims. Who die in flesh alone, & become ghosts, fed on resentment.

You made a ghost of me that lives inside all women born since my time. Whose plight began with mine. You set a precedent when You spat upon my right to turn You down. The men who saw You spit, & watched my punished life, began to chuckle, rubbing hands that itched with ownership. They fancied they were little gods, mortal Apollos, who timed the loving of their women & made mothers out of mates. Chattel, whose hair was worth more than their brains.

Now that predestined fate has given way to self-determination, & meddling in the lives of men no longer is Your Godship's duty   —or prerogative—   You may at long last find the time to hear the plaint of Cassandra, Princess & Prophetess of Troy.

Perhaps Your present ineffective state has made Your Godship ponder the causes of effects. & unless lingering memories of grandeur obstruct Your logic, You may have sought the cause of Your undoing in something You once did. & may have found the seed of Your demotion in Your saliva in my mouth.

I saw Your fall   the fall of all Greek gods   in the lightning flash of Clytemnestra's ax upon my throat, & knew that Your

114

injustice would be justly paid.

Still, Your demise does not mean my
redemption. I could forgive You, & redeem
myself. But Your saliva has congealed into a
cud between my teeth. & between the teeth of
all the women born after me. Who have been
ruminating the right that You denied me. A
woman's right to give or to withhold her body.
Which mortal men in turn denied them.
Making a law of Your example, that forces
women to spread submissive compass legs at a
pressure of their thumbs.

If I forgave You   myself   my worried
mother's coaxing counsel to let You have that
fatal kiss: ... One kiss at least, Cassandra,
daughter, he's after all a God ...   & even
Clytemnestra who was as much as I a
marionette of fate   I'd be anachronistic, a
pagan B.-C. saint.

I'd also set a classical example for
women still alive today to let themselves be
spat upon by slowly shrinking fading gods.
Who will become as ineffective & as
ornamental as You've become, unless I am
redeemed by Your repentance.

In Greek, the word repentance means: a
change of mind. Changing Your mind can
change if not the life You made me live, at
least the legend that I left behind.
Posthumous reputation is still unfair to me.

You'll say that woman's vanity lives on
though she be dead. But Your changed mind
will realize that other women live, & may
believe in You again, if You dispell the
disbelief that met my truth. & still meets
theirs. Your exile has the confines of my
myth.

Your Godship cannot make a comeback

115

unless You first correct the image my name
projects in modern minds. Where I'm made
out to look like the gloom & doom which I
predicted: A madwoman, old before her years.
Wild-eyed & sallow-skinned; one bony arm
raised like a scream. & all around me,
exasperated shrugging Trojans muffle their
ears with their hands, not to hear my ugly
strident voice. —Some even blame the fall of
Troy on me.— While You, the instigator of it
all, continue to evoke untarnished beauty. &
intelligence.

I realize that messengers grow to
resemble the news they bring. & are given
little credit for telling the truth. But You
know as well as I that I was beautiful. Had I
been plain, Your Godship would have devised
some other means than courting me to make
my knowledge worthless.

Forgive me. It's tedious to be reminded
of a dead desire; that was, moreover,
unrequited. Perhaps, had I been plain, a God's
attentions might have flattered me into
submission. But I was as golden & lovely as
Homer says I was. With a voice as sweet as a
songbird's.

But Homer   blind & lyrical   fails to
mention my prophetic gift. Nowhere does he
acknowledge the fact that I foretold the story
he recorded. That I foresaw the long drag of
the siege. Every boring detail of the heroic
slaughter. I recognized Paris as my brother
before Paris himself knew who he was.

Homer was writing five centuries after
the fall, when knowledge had become
unbecoming, for a woman. He could not let
intelligence & beauty share the same female
face, if he desired to be read. He thought that

116

he was being kinder to my memory, making
me beautiful rather than wise.

But without my knowledge I become
unimportant. & banal. Just another beautiful
princess who walked the streets of Troy. A
minor Helen.

Poor Helen. Legend has made of her the
sample type of the new woman that came
about with male supremacy. Placidly
beautiful, without a mind of her own. Open
to the windy choice of men. Of any man, as
long as she was loved. & kept. She has
become the classic femme fatale with whose
defenseless image modern Hellenist pigs still
play their ever-adolescent games of solitaire.

I had decided to defy Your strategy of
competition among women. To be a friend to
Helen when Paris brought her into Troy. It
was an easy task. Helen was excellent
company, soothing & bright, a smiling moon.

I never envied her. Not even when I
foresaw her enviable ample end, peacefully
dying of old age, still worshipped by posterity.
& the bloody horror of mine. Perhaps hers
was a wisdom that I could not share. Because
I saw too much. Or not enough.

How could I blame her for her fate? I'd
read the signs & understood that You would
use the war against my city to denigrate the
female side of life. By severing woman's charm
from woman's mind. Repainting owl-wise
Athena as an old maid.

Did You resent the minds of those who
had withstood Your courtship? Who saw as I
had seen the power greed behind the sunshine
halo of Your smile?

117

& all the others whom You raped &
metamorphosed, yet could not integrate into
Your maleness.

Your Godship's unfulfilled ambitions
streamed together like a flood, at Thetis'
wedding party. When Eris —uninvited—
tossed the contentious apple 'to the Fairest'.
At Your behest?
& was Zeus heeding Your advice when
He decided that a mortal be the judge &
dispatched Hermes down to Paris to have my
estranged brother make the loaded choice He
would not make Himself: between His wife,
His daughters, & His dreams?
You saw Your chance of added power,
watching the losers' rivalry unleash a war
against my city. —Whose walls Your Godship
feigned to be defending while in Odysseus'
fertile mind You sowed the horse-shaped ruse.
You chuckled at the thought of being
worshipped more than Zeus   as the great god
of new civilizations   by men whom You'd
make rulers of the roost, after you banished
womankind from life's decisions.
Your war against a woman's right to
think, so deviously set up, it looked to all
concerned as though a woman were the cause
of man's disaster.
I clearly saw the fall of women once the
walls of Troy came down.
Ironically, Your Godship fell soon after.
Or perhaps not ironically. Perhaps You
overtipped the scale when You enslaved half
of humanity, & passed a law against female
intelligence. Matter weighs more heavily than
mind: it pulled You down.

An alien principle took charge when men began administering nature. When priestesses whose moon-based calendar foretold the cycles with minute precision gave way to priests in women's robes who reckoned by the sun, & left each year awry with one fourth of a useless day.

All forms of life will choke, on earth, leaving no vestige of the Great Apollo, unless You render unto women the right to think & speak their minds   & to be heard   of which You robbed us all the day You spat into my mouth.

Eternally,

Κασσάνδρα

Cassandra

P.S. There always seems to be an apple   & a woman; & a snake   at the beginning of the end. Apollo, after all, means: Appleman. & in Your temples bred the all-knowing whispering sacred serpents.

I never sent the letter.

Perhaps my writing it   assembling it, resentment by resentment, into a three-thousand-year-long mosaic   produced in me the change of mind I recommended to Apollo.

Suddenly he had ceased to matter. I felt relieved of my resentment that had made me impervious to change. I longed to lose the burden of my identity & go back to the source of life, for refreshment.

119

Perhaps my pupa-spirit was at long last heeding the shift from preordination to self-determination that had removed our gods from Olympus & transferred them to museums. I felt much less unique as I scanned through my short shrill life once more, in an unpracticed attempt to assume responsibility. Not for the situations which had confronted me, but for the way I had dealt with them.

—& I don't mean to say that I suddenly felt that I should have given in to Apollo. But perhaps I had given my rejection of him too much importance. & had built my ensuing life on what my mother & Agamemnon used to call: my 'negativity'.

Which I used to call: my truthfulness. My honest rendering of the facts which I foresaw.

Whose moral value I had perhaps overestimated.

Somewhere within my slowly-thawing memory the well-remembered voice of Palamedes seemed to be telling me that
... facts oppress the truth. Which can breathe freely only in poetry & art.

Perhaps my fault was trying to pin truth down, with my predictions.

Which were anything but poetic or artistic. & may have become facts only because of my artless insistence.

Perhaps, if I had worked on giving my knowledge an aesthetic form, my people might

have stayed to listen, & might have learned
their future for the sheer pleasure of my metric
flow. & Troy's & my fate might have been
averted.

All forms of art demand a discipline that
is not unlike praying. That lays a pipeline
between the artist & the truth.
Perhaps our gods themselves would have
approved my style   or envied it   enough to
wish to prove me wrong. & all of us might
have lived better; longer.

LIST OF NAMES

ACHILLES Greek warrior—Seventh & only surviving son of THETIS & PELEUS

AEGISTHUS Lover of CLYTEMNESTRA

AESACUS Son of PRIAM by his first wife ARISBE; half-brother of CASSANDRA—a seer

AGAMEMNON King of Mycena—Husband of CLYTEMNESTRA Leader of the Greek campaign against Troy Lover of CASSANDRA & father of her twin boys PELOPS & TELEDAMUS

AJAX (The Locrian) Greek warrior who rapes CASSANDRA during fall of Troy

ALEXANDRA alternate name of CASSANDRA

ALEXANDER alternate name of CASSANDRA's brother PARIS

ANDROMACHE Wife of HECTOR, sister-in-law of CASSANDRA

ANTENOR Uncle of CASSANDRA (One of the few Trojans to escape—to Italy, where he founded the city of Padua.)

ANTIELUS Greek warrior (who almost spoke inside the wooden horse)

APHRODITE	Roman: VENUS, goddess of love & beauty
APOLLO	Son of ZEUS, god of prophecy/healing/the arts (much of which he took from HERMES)
ARISBE	First—divorced—wife of PRIAM
ASTYNAX	Infant son of HECTOR & ANDROMACHE, nephew of CASSANDRA
ATHENA	Roman: MINERVA, goddess of wisdom & justice—The motherless daughter of ZEUS, sprung from her father's head
BRISEIS	Daughter of the Trojan seer CALCHAS
CALCHAS	Trojan seer—who goes over to the Greeks at the beginning of the war
CASSANDRA	Princess & Prophetess of Troy; Daughter of PRIAM & HECABE
CASTILIA	A woman of Delphi who threw herself down a well to escape APOLLO's advances
CATREUS	of Crete, grandfather of MENELAUS
CHEIRON	A centaur, who raised ACHILLES

CLYTEMNESTRA	Wife of AGAMEMNON; mortal daughter of ZEUS & LEDA; sister of HELEN
COREBUS	Prince of Phrygia, one of CASSANDRA's suitors
CREUSA	Daughter of PRIAM & HECABE, older sister of CASSANDRA
CRONUS	Roman: SATURN
DAPHNE	A nymph—who changed herself into a laurel in order to escape APOLLO's advances
DEIDAMEIA	Daughter of King LYCOMEDES of Scyros; mother of ACHILLES' son NEOPTOLEMUS
DEIPHOBUS	Son of PRIAM & HECABE; brother of CASSANDRA; husband of HELEN after PARIS' death
DIOMEDES	Greek warrior, friend of ODYSSEUS
ERIS	Goddess of discord
ERINNYS	The Furies
EURYPYLUS	of Mysia; cousin & fiance of CASSANDRA
GAIA	The Great Mother—Earth as the basic goddess
GANYMEDE	Nephew of CASSANDRA's grandfather LAOMEDON—cup bearer to ZEUS

HECABE	Queen of Troy—Second wife of PRIAM; mother of CASSANDRA
HECTOR	Trojan warrior—Oldest son of PRIAM & HECABE (although perhaps a son of APOLLO?); oldest brother of CASSANDRA; husband of ANDROMACHE
HELEN	Daughter of ZEUS & LEDA— Queen of Sparta—wife of MENELAUS; PARIS, DEIPHOBUS (et al.?)
HELENUS	Son of PRIAM & HECABE; twin brother of CASSANDRA; seer, who goes over to the Greek camp toward end of war
HERA	Roman: JUNO, sister & second wife of ZEUS
HERACLES	HERCULES
HERMES	Roman: MERCURY, the messenger of the gods
HERMIONE	Daughter of HELEN & MENELAUS
HESIONE	Sister of PRIAM, CASSANDRA's aunt—booty, & perhaps wife, of TELAMON
ILUS	The builder of Troy— CASSANDRA's greatgrandfather
IPHIGENEIA	Oldest daughter of AGAMEMNON & CLYTEMNESTRA (Rumored daughter of HELEN with THESEUS)

LAOCOON	Seer & priest of APOLLO
LAODICE	Daughter of PRIAM & HECABE— Older sister of CASSANDRA
LAOMEDON	Father of PRIAM—CASSANDRA's grandfather
LYCOMEDES	King of Scyros (who hid ACHILLES among his daughters)
MENELAUS	King of Sparta—Brother of AGAMEMNON—Husband of HELEN, father of.HERMIONE
MESTOR	Son of PRIAM—half brother of CASSANDRA
MOPSUS	Great seer—son of TIRESIAS' daughter MANTO
NAUPLIUS	Father of PALAMEDES
NEOPTOLEMUS	Son of ACHILLES & DEIDAMEIA— Greek warrior particularly active in the sack of Troy
ODYSSEUS	ULYSSES—Greek warrior— Husband of PENELOPE
OENONE	Fountain nymph, first lover (wife?) of PARIS
ORESTES	Son of AGAMEMNON & CLYTEMNESTRA —first matricide to be acquitted—in Athens

OTHRYNEUS	A suitor of CASSANDRA
PALAMEDES	Greek warrior—Inventor, philosopher, & prophet
PALLAS	Playmate of ATHENA
PARIS	(ALEXANDER)—second son of PRIAM & HECABE, older brother of CASSANDRA—Husband of HELEN (& perhaps of OENONE)
PATROCLUS	Cousin & adored friend of ACHILLES
PELEUS	Mortal husband of THETIS— father of ACHILLES
PELOPS	One of CASSANDRA's twin sons by AGAMEMNON
PENELOPE	Wife of ODYSSEUS; cousin of HELEN
PENTHESILEIA	Queen of the Amazons (Her corpse was shamefully abused & mutilated by ACHILLES)
PHOENIX	King of Molossia
POLITES	Son of PRIAM & HECABE, brother of CASSANDRA
POLYXENA	Daughter of PRIAM & HECABE, sister of CASSANDRA
POSEIDON	Roman: NEPTUNE—water god; brother of ZEUS

PRIAM	(Initially named: PODARES)—King of Troy, husband of HECABE, father of CASSANDRA
PROMETHEUS	Martyred for stealing fire for human use—(His sons' tombs were in Troy.)
PYRRHA	Girl's name given to ACHILLES while in hiding at LYCOMEDES' court in Scyros
PYTHON	Female serpent, the initial occupant of the oracle of Delphi, slain by APOLLO
SINOPE	A nymph wronged by APOLLO
TELAMON	Friend & ally of HERACLES—Husband (or conqueror) of CASSANDRA's aunt HESIONE
TELEDAMUS	Twin son of CASSANDRA by AGAMEMNON
THEMIS	Daughter of GAIA; first wife of ZEUS
THETIS	Daughter of the RIVER; granddaughter of the OCEAN; wife of PELEUS, mother of ACHILLES
TIRESIAS	The greatest of all Greek seers
TROILUS	Youngest son of PRIAM & HECABE (or perhaps APOLLO & HECABE); younger brother of CASSANDRA
ZEUS	Roman: JUPITER

PS3525 02152 A9
 +The autobiograph+Molinaro, Ursule

0 00 02 0205325 2
MIDDLEBURY COLLEGE